MO...
DAISY PRESCOTT

NEXT TO YOU

A LOVE WITH ALTITUDE NOVEL

DAISY PRESCOTT

Cover Design by ©SM Lumetta

Editing: There for You Editing

Proofreading: Proofing Style

Interior Design & Formatting: Type A Formatting

To my readers who fell for the
charming bartender with a man bun.

ONE

STAN

I HEAR THE crunch of bone against bone before pain radiates from my ankle, buckling me to the ground in agony.

The mountain officially closed three weeks ago, but tell that to a bunch of wild rugby players who think we're invincible. Nothing can take us down or stop us once we set our minds to something.

No lifts? We'll hike to the top with our boots and skis tied to our backpacks. Snow the consistency of a frozen margarita? It's still snow. Snow means skiing or boarding whenever possible. Who cares if there are rocks poking out and bare spots. Be a man. Ski over them.

The irony is I made it down the mountain without an issue. After taking off my ski boots, I switched to hiking boots. The ones with great traction.

Traction didn't save me from the rock I tripped over that landed me flat on my arse.

A *bliksemes* rock.

Not even a boulder.

The damn thing was loose from the spring melt. It slid and

I slipped.

Right into the base of a tree.

My ego and pride are lying in the mud while the assholes I call teammates laugh at me.

"How does it feel to be taken down by a goliath?" Logan asks between snorts. "Now you know how the rest of us feel when we face off against you on the pitch."

"*Vokkof.*" Taking a deep breath, I brace myself on my left leg to stand. All right, not too bad being vertical again. Feeling cocky, I test out the other ankle.

"*Vokken kak, naai, vok, moerskont,*" I curse a storm in Afrikaans.

Stars, stripes, triangles, and a vortex of whirling pain spin behind my eyes when I attempt to put weight on my right foot.

"Impressive cursing, Barnyard." Motherfucking Easley thinks he's a riot with that wholly unoriginal nickname for my last name Barnard.

"*Ek gaan vir jou n poesklap gee.*" I threaten to slap the shit out of him. "*Thula man.*"

"At least you didn't hit the tree with your pretty face. Think of all the money you'd lose."

I have a pretty face. Sue me. Or better yet, complain to my parents. It's their genetics to blame. Somehow over the years of playing rugby, I've never had my nose broken or earned a scar.

I wouldn't mind a scar for character. Tell people I got it in a knife fight or a shark encounter. Something to toughen up my pretty boy image.

"Lee, you okay? You're looking a little green."

"Honestly, I'm thinking about puking right now." *Vokken kak. Fucking shit.*

Logan takes a giant step back, slips in the mud, and falls on his arse. Good.

"Listen, one of you mind driving me to the hospital?"

"No walking it off?" Easley hands me one of my ski poles.

It's not crutches, but it'll have to do. Logan and Easley pick up my gear and follow as I hobble down the small slope to the parking lot.

I find my keys in the backpack and toss them to Logan.

"You're going to let me drive the Rover? You sure you didn't hit your head?"

"I'll be in the backseat, watching and judging your every move." I open the back passenger door and awkwardly hop inside, trying to not knock my ankle against anything. The tightness of my boot tells me my ankle is swelling rapidly.

Logan drives like an old woman while Easley gives him shit as his co-pilot. Every turn and bump in the road on the short drive from Buttermilk to the hospital shoots stabs of pain up my leg.

I'm almost hoping it's a break and not a torn ligament or severe sprain. Bones heal better and faster.

How am I supposed to train for the summer rugby season if I can't walk?

Given it's the start of the off-season, the hospital is quiet for a Wednesday. The bunch of us are pretty well known around here for the contusions, scrapes and dislocated shoulders we get during rugby season. Being a ski town, broken bones and torn ligaments are standard procedure for the emergency docs.

I send the guys away while I wait for an exam and X-rays. No need for them to linger around like mother ducks. One of them can leave my car at the condo's garage. Even if I only sprained my ankle, I won't be able to drive. Hopefully I'll be on some amazing painkillers and won't care.

Three hours later I exit with a pretty black boot on my leg, the worst pair of crutches ever, a script for pain pills, and instructions to stay off the ankle for six weeks.

Total number of broken bones: two. Not counting the hairline fracture in my fibula. Non-weight bearing, it doesn't count. I've played with hairline fractures before.

I'm Goliath taken down by a rock.

The hospital calls a cab for me. Stoner Darren shows up, a hemp and patchouli scented cloud spilling out the side door of the mini-van when he opens it for me.

"Thanks, D."

"Man, what'd you do?"

"Broke my ankle."

"Skiing?"

"Kind of." I stare out the window at the brown mountains and bare aspen trees. Technically not summer, the first week of May is closer to winter here in the Rockies. Hell, we could ski more if we get a freak June or July snow. It's snowed on the 4th of July before.

Stranger things have happened.

Darren offers to run into the drug store to pick up my pain pills. The Vicodin they gave me in the ER works nicely, but will wear off soon. It also makes me drowsy. My lids feel heavy, so I let my eyes close while I wait for Darren in the warm car.

I should call my mum to let her know I'm injured but okay.

Then again, she'll worry I'm lying, like the time in university when I was concussed and told her it was only a flesh wound. She missed the Monty Python joke and flew to see me the next day.

It's an even longer flight from Cape Town to Aspen.

I spoke to her a few weeks ago for her birthday, so I owe her a call.

My father won't care. He'll tell me to toughen up and work harder. If he answers his phone. Otherwise his secretary will act sympathetic, and send a card with a forged signature, which will arrive weeks late.

Not worth the bother even if he is closer in Chicago instead of half a world away.

With a confused jolt, I wake up when Darren tosses my prescription bag into my lap.

"You should consider becoming a nurse, Darren. You have a real gift for empathizing with people's plights and pains." I sit up, forgetting about my ankle until the pain reminds me why I'm napping in the back of Darren's van.

"Why do you think I've driven a cab all these years? For the big bucks? Nah, I love people. L-o-v-e love them all."

"You love the tips and money the same as me. Do I want to be making fancy cocktails for people all my life?"

"I thought you were one of the glitterati." Darren smirks at me through the rearview mirror. "Athlete, model, scion . . ."

Frowning at the "scion" label, I accidentally shift my ankle and grimace from the pain. "You've been reading my press releases again. I'm flattered."

My father, who also happens to be my former manager, put out press releases the way some parents sent Christmas letters bragging over every mundane accomplishment their children achieved over the course of the year. Only his were more impersonal and full of exaggerated half-truths. One had my age wrong by two years.

His bragging slowed when I chose to go to university instead of playing rugby professionally. The press releases stopped around the same time I moved to Aspen.

There is a reason I live in Aspen year round. Actually, there are many, but in regards to my father, he hates the mountains.

Everything about them: the cold, the height, the thin air. The roads are too windy, the flights too bumpy, and the hotels too short. My father prefers to look down on the rest of the world, not be intimidated by nature. Complain, complain, complain.

If it keeps him away, I'll live here forever.

When we arrive at my condo, I see the Rover parked in front of the garage. The numskulls couldn't follow simple directions.

A light snow begins falling as I exit the backseat with my crutches and goody bag from the pharmacy. I thank Darren for the ride and over-tip him. No matter how much he claims to love people, the man barely scrapes by.

Word is he lives in a trailer down valley. Probably of his own choosing. He could be a millionaire hoarder or something. Stranger things have happened in Woody Creek, former home of Hunter S. Thompson. That's all anyone needs to know about the area.

I'm now thinking about all the drugs Hunter probably did over his lifetime. I wonder what peyote feels like. Or LSD. Or mushrooms. Or cocaine.

Working as a bartender in a high-end hotel means I've seen a lot of things. Some unimaginable to most people. Been offered designer drugs, sex, invites to threesomes, foursomes, full-blown orgies, to be kept, to be flown to Dubai. It's crazy what people think money can buy them. Everything and everyone has a price.

Wow. I'm really high and philosophical right now.

Music blasts from my neighbor's condo. I lean against the wall in between our front doors, resting my shoulder on the rustic wood siding. The rough texture fascinates me, so I run my hand over the bumps and knots. My crutch slips out of my grip, falling into the door with a crash.

The music pauses and I hear footsteps approaching. Why is someone inside my house? I reach for my keys, dropping the other crutch. Now standing on one foot, my head on the door and my shoulder braced on the jamb, I almost fall over when the door swings opens.

"Sage? What are you doing in my house? Are you stealing my biscuits again?"

My beautiful, ethereal next-door neighbor is wearing tiny yoga shorts and a loose sweatshirt, which falls off her shoulder, revealing the absence of any evidence of a bra. To confirm this, I let my gaze settle below her collarbone.

No bra, but the material is too thick to see much more than the small swoop of her breasts. I'll need to move the fabric out of the way to have a peek. My hand lifts and I watch it move toward the neckline with an out-of-body feeling.

I might be having an out-of-body experience. Sage and I have lived next door to each other for two years. She's one of the few women friends I have in Aspen who I haven't slept with or hasn't tried to seduce me. I could even say she's one of the few friends I have here. Period.

A soft cough and a gentle hand on my arm make me pause.

"Hey Stan. Eyes up here. Are you high?" She steps forward, but trips on something. Looking down, she asks, "What's with the crutches?"

I blink at her a few times. "Crutches?"

When she bends over, I have a straight view down her shirt and get confirmation she is most definitely not wearing a bra. Her movement is too fast to get more than a glimpse.

"Lee?"

"You always call me Stan, not Lee." I focus on her face. Her brow is scrunched up and her lips are pursed in a pout.

"Are you okay?" I like her voice. It's soft, and has a solid American accent from the Midwest. I think.

"I like your accent."

"Said no one ever about a Midwest accent. Come inside."

"I broke my ankle."

Her thin arms wraps around my waist. "I can see your boot. That explains the crutches. The hospital sent you home by yourself?"

"I didn't drive. Darren gave me a ride home. Landon and Easley parked my car in the driveway when I asked them to put it in the garage. They kind of suck as friends."

She laughs. "No comment."

"Why did you ever go out with Landon? He's not good enough for you."

"Come on, inside." She push-pulls me toward the open door.

"Not until you tell me why him." Landon's fine for a mate, but he's a womanizer and a prick. "He's not good enough for you."

"You already said that. Where were you last year with this brilliant advice when I went out with him?"

I take a step and remember my boot. "I need my crutches."

She hands them to me, and I hop over the threshold. Leading me to the small living room, she fluffs the extra pillows on her couch and pats the cushion. "Sit down."

I obey her bossy orders. "You should have asked me about Landon. I would've told you he's an arsehole."

"So you've said. Repeatedly. After he broke up with me."

I slump down on the couch and rest my bad ankle on the end. "You need a longer couch."

"You're funny today." She puts a crazy patterned rainbow pillow under my boot.

"I'm stoned. They gave me some shot at the hospital."

"I can tell."

I remember the bag from the pharmacy. "I have more drugs. Darren got them for me."

"I'm going to assume you mean prescriptions and not the other stuff Stoner Darren can get you."

"Have you ever done peyote? I've never done any of the good drugs."

With a chuckle, she walks a few feet away to the kitchen counter and then to the sink.

I watch her move around. She's *vokken* graceful and beautiful. Landon is a stupid prat. "Why did you go out with Landon and not me? I'm much nicer and better looking than he is."

Her sweatshirt slips farther off her shoulder as she brings me a glass of water.

I reach up and touch her exposed skin. "So soft."

"I, um . . ." She coughs. "Do you need anything? Soup?"

"I'm not sick. Broken bone." I lift my booted leg. "Remember?"

Because she's close and I'm curious, I touch the skin of her leg to see if it's as soft as her shoulder. "Your leg is soft, too."

"That tickles." She giggles and steps out of reach. "I'll make you some soup. Probably good for you to eat if you're on pain meds, which clearly you are."

I lie back against the pillows. From here I can watch her move around her small kitchen. Our condos are the same layout, only mirrored. Hers feels more like a home. Mine has the same furniture I inherited from the guy who rented it previously. Although I did get a new mattress. I'm not a complete beast.

"You changed your hair." Sage has pale blond hair and she's always adding streaks of color to it. This week her ends are pink in the front like she dipped them in punch.

She lifts a lock and examines it. "I did. I used Kool Aid this time."

"I like it."

"Glad to hear you approve. Give it a week and it'll be

different again."

"Different is good. Different makes you beautiful."

I barely hear her soft giggle. "I like you on drugs. You're very sweet and complimentary."

I grumble and shift on the couch. "I'm always sweet."

"When you need something or you've turned on the charm at the bar. Otherwise you're quiet—the strong, silent type."

Now I'm pouting. "I'm always nice to you. We're friends."

"That we are." She takes a bowl out of the cupboard. "Soup's done."

I sit up more when she brings over the bowl, a cloth napkin, and a spoon. I expect her to hand me the napkin, but instead she tucks it over my shirt. The gesture is something my mother would've done for me when I was little. I miss my mother.

I should call her. I'm feeling nostalgic and homesick for a place I haven't lived in years. Emotions make me vulnerable. My father gave me that advice when I began playing rugby seriously at fifteen. I need to stop with the mushy emotions and toughen up.

It's only a hairline fracture, nothing to cry over.

"You're not going to feed me, too, are you? I think I can manage a spoon." My voice holds an edge to it.

Sage flinches slightly. "I'm not making airplane noises even if you beg."

She curls up in the old leather armchair at the other end of the couch. Now she's too far away, which also makes me cranky.

I slurp the soup, testing to make sure it's no too hot. "Do you have crackers? I love crumbled saltines in my tomato soup."

"So demanding." Her smile returns as she searches for crackers. "You'll have to survive with Ritz."

I hold up my bowl for her to add the crackers. "Make sure to break them up really well."

She obliges with a sigh, but I can see in her eyes I amuse her. "Thank you."

"You're welcome. How did it happen?"

In between spoonfuls, I tell her the embarrassing story about being taken down by a rock.

"At least you weren't alone when it happened. Imagine the shit you would get from ski patrol for having to be rescued from the parking lot."

"It was the base of the bunny hill." I defend myself.

"Right, that's so much better." She grins at me. "I'm never letting you forget this when you tease me about not skiing double-black diamond runs with you."

I don't like being teased by anyone, but I'd take it from her. The soup and drugs combine to make me sleepy. I place the empty bowl on the coffee table before closing my eyes.

"You're so good to me, Sage."

"I know. I'll even let you nap on my couch, but try not to drool on the pillows."

I shift around, getting more comfortable. With my eyes still closed I feel a soft blanket being settled over me. It smells of lavender and something girly and pretty.

"If you want to date me, all you need to do is say the word. I'd never let you go." My thoughts become words as I feel myself being dragged under a wave of sleep.

TWO

SAGE

LEE SNORES ON my sofa.

Man bun sporting, too gorgeous to exist in the real world Lee Barnard is drooling on my throw pillow right this very minute. While I stare at his scruffy profile, he parts his beautiful, pouty lips. Women would kill for his lip color or to find the perfect shade of deep rose. His mouth is a thing of beauty.

Not only his mouth. All of him. The complete package. Not that I've seen his package. I've gone to enough rugby matches in the summer to get a vague idea that all of him is perfect.

Unlike Landon Roberts who should come with a label about false advertising. He needs one of those car mirror stickers that warn objects may appear larger than they really are.

What can I say? I was a silly twenty-three year old. Now as a wise twenty-four year old, I'd never fall for his lines and slick moves.

Naïve Midwest girl getting charmed out of her panties wouldn't make the local paper. It's a story as old as the Rockies.

Heart-dented and wiser, I avoid the hot-shot guys around town. No rugby players in the summer. No snow-boarders in the winter. No bartenders. No white water rafting guys or fly-fishermen. No guides. Definitely no cowboys.

I've basically ruled out every eligible single guy in the Roaring Fork Valley. Perhaps the entire state of Colorado.

There must be a solid, stable banker or accountant I haven't met yet. A fireman could be responsible.

Lee snort-snores and shifts under the blanket. I cup my chin in my hands and continue staring at him. His profile could be carved in marble for future generations to admire. Maybe not the man bun though.

I liked it when he started growing out his hair, but he took it too far when he shaved the underside and began stealing my ponytail holders. The soft waves balances the strong angles of his face. With messy hair, he looks more human and less like a fallen angel.

However, the bun makes him look like a samurai wannabe. A ninja who has extremely poor ninja skills. An oversized top-knot quail.

For a brief moment, I contemplate pulling a Delilah and cutting off the bun with one clean snip. But unlike stealing Samson's strength, I think I'd be cursing myself. Lee does not need to be more handsome.

I don't need more women falling all over him.

It was my idea that he should go by Stan at work. Stan and Stanley are the least sexiest names. Right up there with Herbert and Ernie.

Then the man bun happened and in my head I started calling him "Stan the Man Bun". Amazingly, that helped make him normal. I could be friends with a guy named Stan while silently lusting after Lee, the unattainable.

Amazing what a name can do.

Bonus because when I think of Stan/Lee, I think of the

comic book legend. He's a genius, but way too old for me. Unlike Lee who is twenty-seven and perfectly perfect in every way. Even while snoring.

My carefully constructed defenses now lie scattered around the living room as I take inventory of his perfections. Tall with long legs, he barely fits on my seven-foot sofa. His broad shoulder hangs over the edge. One strong arm is flung behind his head while his other forearm rests across a hidden six-pack. Long fingers sprawl across his thick upper thigh. Damn baggy ski pants hide anything else of interest.

Stan showing up high and chatty is more than adorable. I make mental notes of all the things to tease him about at a future date.

Then *kapow.*

He tells me I'm beautiful and caresses my shoulder. Are shoulders even erogenous zones? They should be. Mine clearly are.

One gentle touch and my body lights up like the sky during a nighttime thunderstorm.

I trace my fingers over the skin he called soft, trying to recapture the sensation. Nothing. I know it's not the location, but the man behind the touch.

I felt more from a shoulder caress than anything I ever did from another man's touch. Could be I'm starved for affection.

I get massages all the time. I trade barre classes with Zoe for them. Sadly, her strong hands aren't the same as a man's touch. I should try to do an exchange with a male massage therapist.

Most year round residents work a barter system to afford living in Aspen or Snowmass. Especially during the off-season when bookings slow and tips dwindle to nothing.

Anyone who can afford it takes off for a quick vacation in the sun or goes home to visit family in between the seasons.

Not me. At least not until the end of July. Same for Zoe. We're both from Chicago, but she and her boyfriend, Neil, moved out here last fall once he finished his MBA at Northwestern.

I should ask Neil if he knows any boring banker types. He probably does.

Summer season will begin in June and bring with it a new flood of tourists. Different from the winter visitors, summer people are more outdoorsy and autonomous. Some come for the music tent and ballet school, but most are adventure types.

Years ago, I spent a summer in Aspen dancing ballet. Still in high school, it was my first taste of freedom and feeling like an adult. It's probably the reason I returned here after college.

That and the free rent at my parents' condo. Both were disappointed I didn't major in business and promise to take over their home goods retail empire. I'm happy to let my sister and her MBA sporting husband be the third generation to run Bloom and Board. My grandfather started with a single store in Evanston, selling housewares out of crates and simple modern furniture he designed himself. Now in every state and several countries overseas, Bloom and Board is a lifestyle brand.

Stan moans in his sleep and his face contorts. I glance at the clock on the microwave. He's been asleep for an hour. I have no idea when he last took any pain meds. I've never played nurse before. I can barely manage to keep myself alive.

I work two jobs and volunteer with an animal rescue organization down valley. Not only dogs and cats, we foster horses, donkeys, and several pygmy goats on the ranch. Last summer a hawk with a broken wing did some rehab with us before being set free again.

Mom loves to ask me when I'm going to be a real adult. Dad teases me about how much rental income he loses every year I stay here. Trust me, he doesn't need the extra money.

My response is always the same: cut me off if they want. I haven't touched my trust fund despite gaining access to it earlier this year.

With the barre classes and working in the lingerie shop on commission, I make enough to not need roommates. My two bedroom condo is more room than I need, but my family has a bedroom if they come to visit. Ever. Mom had a bout of altitude sickness three years ago and swore off the mountains for a beach house in the Hamptons. Dad never skis anymore and complains about his bad knees from "real skiing" on moguls back in the eighties.

Lee, I mean Stan, never talks about his family or how he can afford to live alone. I guess he makes enough from bartending and modeling jobs he gets around here. I'm sure being the face of the ski company's ad campaign helps.

Helps get him more women. I really try to ignore female laughter or other girl sounds through our shared wall. I do. I've become excellent at tuning out things with music or the TV.

Who can blame them for their enthusiasm and excitement? I bet they don't even have a problem calling him Stan or Lee, or even Stan Lee, and still finding him sexy.

Obviously.

The accent alone melts clothing. He can crank it up or sound almost American when he wants.

The man, the myth, opens his eyes and stares back at me.

He mumbles something and wipes his mouth. "Have I been drooling?"

"Horribly. You owe me a new pillow."

His pale blue eyes widen and he looks embarrassed as his cheeks redden.

"Anything else? Talk in my sleep? Did I say anything odd?" Sleep deepens his voice and strengthens his normally faint accent. I file this information away in my folder of "Things I know about Lee Barnard".

"Not really odd. You professed your love for me and saltine crackers. I'm not sure I'm the polyamorous type, but I'm still considering your proposal."

"What?" He shifts and grimaces. His skin pales with pain as he clenches his jaw.

I'm up and out of my chair to refill his glass before he can ask. For a few seconds I struggle with the human-proof lid on the pill bottle.

"Here, let me." He stills my fingers and takes the container, easily opening the container.

I stare at his Adam's apple as he swallows. I find the oddest things about him to be sexy. Protruding vocal chords are hot when they're his.

"Thanks for letting me crash here. I should head home." He sits up and I stop him with a hand on his shoulder.

"You probably shouldn't be alone. What if you have an undiagnosed head injury?"

"Other than my bruised ego, my head is fine. I don't want to take over your space."

"It's okay. You can stay." I swallow. "I like having you here."

He studies me from the corner of his eye. "That's not what you usually say. How many times have you told me to take my 'guy stink' home to my own place?"

It's true. I have said those exact words many times. "Only when you show up and sit your sweaty self on my leather chair. No one wants to sit on leather soaked in Stan juice."

He gives me a cocky smile. "I'm claiming it as my own."

"You have enough furniture already."

"Maybe I'm marking my territory to keep your other suitors away."

"Ha! It must be working."

He grins. Cocky bastard. "Having a bit of a dry spell?"

"Sahara."

"Side effect from your terrible taste in men? I told you Landon wasn't good enough for you."

"Thanks for the reminder. For the third time today."

He cocks his head. "I told you that earlier? I don't remember."

"Right before the declaration of cracker love. You were on a tirade about poor Landon being unworthy of my affections. As if I needed to be reminded. I'm the one who dated him."

He grumbles and I swear the sound reverberates around in his chest like a growl.

"As part of my end of season resolution, I've sworn off all rugby players, ski instructors, snowboarders, ski patrol—basically all men within driving distance."

He looks genuinely disappointed at my new oath. "Seems a shame to let Landon ruin you for the good guys."

"I'm open to someone who works in an office, draws a salary, and has full medical benefits; dental and eye coverage would be bonuses."

"Sounds boring as hell."

"Exactly."

He stares, scrutinizing me with his cool blue eyes. "You're hardly the boring type. Don't settle for average when you're extraordinary."

His eyes unsettle me more than his words.

"Did they give you truth serum at the hospital instead of morphine?"

"I'm not stoned. I'm trying to be honest." He pauses before adding, "Friend to friend."

I nod. Friends.

There's no convincing Stan to stay the night. I make him

promise to text me if he needs anything or falls over and can't get up. As we say an awkward goodnight at the door, I tell him I'll be over in the morning.

"Be sure to knock before letting yourself in with your key. I might be sleeping naked." His wink tells me he's joking. I think.

I laugh it off while picturing him naked. It's sexy until I imagine him sans clothes standing there with his big gray boot cast.

I wake up early with a plan to surprise Stan. I make blueberry muffins from a box mix, following the instructions for high altitude. After a few disasters over the years, I've learned box mixes are my friends.

I don't bother to brush my hair or put on makeup. The messy pink bun on my head matches my sweater. Plaid slippers cover my feet below my standard black leggings.

Holding a large travel mug of coffee, a smaller one with milk, and the plate of muffins balanced on my arm, I knock on his door with an elbow. I'm hoping he's awake. After a few minutes of waiting, I set down the coffee and ring the doorbell.

From inside I hear his voice and another voice. When the door opens, I'm expecting Stan, not naked, but at least tousled and gorgeous from sleep.

Instead, a slim brunette greets me. She's completely put together, not a hair out of place, wearing pale gray leggings and a long white cashmere tunic. Only cashmere could appear so soft and fluffy. At least she doesn't look like she woke up and rolled out of Stan's bed to answer the door. I'm pretty certain he doesn't own a flat iron.

"Aren't you the sweetest?" Her sarcastic tone disagrees with her spoken words. "Lee's already had breakfast and coffee. I brought it over first thing this morning. I would've stayed the night with him if he let me know he was injured. No man should be left alone with a broken leg."

"Ankle fracture. Hairline fracture in his ankle."

She ignores my correction and continues cooing about the poor thing and how she's so glad she's here to take care of him.

The man in question appears behind her on his crutches. Dreams do come true when I realize his hair is out of the man bun and a beautiful mess framing his face in dark waves.

"Sage!" He sounds happy to see me. His guest blocks him from getting any closer on his crutches.

She studies me like a hawk eyeing a piece of meat thrown into its enclosure. Trapped into playing nice, she's not thrilled about it. Dreams of pecking my eyes out probably dance behind her perfectly mascaraed and lined eyes.

"I'd invite you in if Tess ever moved out of the way." He rests his weight on both crutches and taps her shoulder from behind.

This snaps her out of her thoughts—probably of me vanishing before her eyes—and she gives me a cold smile. Calling it a smile is a stretch. She shows me her teeth.

My, what sharp teeth you have.

The better to bite off your face, my dear.

She reluctantly moves out of my way, still positioning herself between Stan and me.

"You baked?" He grabs for the plate, forgetting his crutches.

"It's from a box." I'm not sure why I need to downplay the effort. "I'll put them on your counter."

Spread out on his island is an array of muffins, pastries, and other foods from Paradise Bakery. I recognize their signature almond croissant. My favorite.

Next to the array of perfect baked goods, my muffins look pitiful.

Tell that to Stan. He has half of one consumed already. I'm

surprised he hasn't eaten the paper, too.

"There's something about homemade," he mumbles around a mouthful of muffin. "Thanks, Sage."

Feeling more confident, I face the brunette. "We haven't met. I'm Sage."

"Tess."

"Tess. Sage. Sage. Tess," Stan says between bites. "Sage lives next door."

"Oh, how nice. You're the next-door neighbor." Tess smiles for real this time. I've been categorized as a non-threat.

"Very. You know what they say about location, location, location."

Her left eye twitches. "Lee and I work together at the resort. Long hours all week. It's great to get along so well with someone who I spend so much time with."

Point received.

"Funny, we've never met. I'm there all the time. You don't look familiar."

Stan happily eats another muffin, either knowingly avoiding the brewing cat fight or completely oblivious to the tension simmering women in front of him.

I have zero claim to him, but I can tell Tess is no good. Trusting my instincts with this one. For once.

"Sage teaches barre classes at the hotel among other places. You should take her class. She looks like a princess, but she's a sadist under the pink hair." Stan smiles at me with approval.

Tess observes us with thinly contained contempt. Or maybe it's hunger. Her typical Aspen ski bunny outfit reveals her size zero body.

I'm fit, but I never get below a size six. Next to her chicken legs, I'm curvy. She could probably shop in the mall store for promiscuous tweens. Most likely she does.

"You should take a class sometime. If you work at the resort, you get a discount." I'd love to make her sweat and inflict a little pain.

"Oh, I never workout. I'm blessed with being naturally thin." She eyes the carb buffet longingly.

Uh huh, sure.

"Mind if I grab something?" I ask Stan, not Tess.

He hands me the almond croissant. "I know you want this one."

"You know me so well." We're sharing a moment. Until Tess coils herself around his arm.

"Shouldn't you be elevating your leg? Come over to the couch and I'll make you snuggly and comfy-cozy."

I arch an eyebrow at her baby talk. Stan shrugs and follows her. "I should. Sage, will you bring over the muffins?"

I don't bother to set any aside and bring him the entire plate. "There's coffee too."

Tess busies herself with tucking a thick knit blanket around his legs, spending a little too much attention to smoothing it over his stomach. He stops her hand from going any farther south into the land of inappropriate work colleague touching.

I know Stan. He doesn't "date" coworkers. He's more the type to indulge in a weekend or weeklong dalliance. Love and be left seems to be his motto. He's never the bad guy if they have to fly away home after a few days.

I've done the same thing to scratch an itch or two. Handsome guy comes here to ski or snowboard. Flirts, charms, seduces, and most importantly, leaves.

It's the circle of life in resort towns whether they be at the beach, desert, or mountains.

The transient nature draws people like me here. Nothing feels permanent. Or too complicated. Sometimes people find real love. Maybe do the long distance thing for a few months, then someone moves. Typically, it's the person who lives here who moves back to the real world. Tough to find jobs and affordable housing if you want to be a real adult in a resort town.

Tess now perches on the arm of Stan's sofa. Her cooing and fussing continue as she breaks off a piece of muffin to hand to him.

It's enough to push me toward the door.

I recall my upbringing and with a bright, fake smile, excuse myself. "Lovely to meet you, Tess. Stan, text me if you need anything. I'm working at the shop today, but can lock up for a few minutes if you want something."

"I thought you said you were a barre instructor." Tess pouts her glossy lips in confusion and suspicion.

"I can only teach so many classes a week. I work at Cheeks part time."

Her eyes light up when I say the name. Cheeks is legendary in town for the best lingerie and elegant toys, or as the owner prefers to call them "pleasure enhancers".

"Ooh, do you get an employee discount?" Tess practically purrs. Now I'll be her best friend.

"We're having an end of season sale starting this week."

She lets her gaze settle on Stan's midsection for a beat before licking her lips. Her actions remind me of a cat toying with a mouse.

"Maybe I'll have to stop by later and pick up something new." She touches his non-broken ankle. "What's your favorite color, Lee?"

Stan chokes and coughs around the bite of muffin in his mouth. His glacial blue eyes meet mine. He widens them for a second, letting me know he's aware of Tess's intentions. With a quick wink, he replies, "Pink."

THREE

STAN

I SAY THE first color I see.

Pink.

I could've answered sage green, but I'm thankful my brain is working despite the pain pills.

That would've been too obvious. Saying pink is generic, expected.

"I look fabulous in pink. Red, too." Tess touches my leg again.

She can drop the subtle and coy acting. Offering to blow me behind the bar one night as I was closing up kind of ruins the innocent angle she's attempting now.

I turned her down. I should've turned down her offer to bring over breakfast this morning after she covered my shift last night. At least I was coherent enough in the ER to text the group chat about my shift. She was the first to respond.

I rarely listen to my father about anything, but he did teach me to never get involved with my coworkers. He brilliantly had an affair with his secretary. She sued him for sexual harassment. Really good parenting to lead by example like that.

Whatever my father does, I do the opposite. See how smart I am?

I've told Tess she's off limits. She thinks this means she's too good for me. It's easy to let her believe it. She's nice and pretty, but not worth getting fired over for shagging at work.

The way her face lit up over Sage's job at Cheeks tells me she still hopes I'll see her in her bra and knickers.

I've never visited Sage at work. My hippie, free spirit neighbor surrounded by all sorts of naughty things might destroy whatever resolve holds up my illusion of platonic feelings toward her.

If a quick, colleague provided blow job is off limits, there needs to be a new definition of forbidden for my next door neighbor.

In another teachable moment: Dad had an affair with Mum's best friend, who happened to live next door to us at the time.

Thanks, Dad.

Not that I'm a monk. Flirting is my favorite sport after rugby. I train hard to be good at rugby. Flirting comes effortlessly. I adore a good banter with a beautiful or confident woman.

Giving as good as she gets can make any woman—old, young, pretty, plain, attractive—come across as confident and sexy. Seeing a fire ignite in an older woman's eyes is more interesting to me than perky tits being shoved across the bar.

Flirting is an art. Unlike youth, which is a temporary gravity defying feat.

I've been known to flirt with anything with a pulse. It's a talent.

Doesn't hurt my tips either.

"Shit."

Two pairs of eyes watch me, waiting for an explanation.

"How am I supposed to bartend on crutches?"

Sage frowns. "You'll have to get someone to cover you for a few weeks."

"I volunteer!" Tess pats my booted ankle in her enthusiasm.

I moan as a sharp pain follows.

She apologizes. "I mean, the champagne bar on the mountain is closed for the season now. I could pick up some extra shifts in the lounge."

Pouring champagne is different than crafting signature cocktails. Somehow I think Tess could pour cranberry and vodka all night and still convince everyone she's the best.

"I'll call Drew and let him know I'm out." I'm dreading having to replay the rock story.

"You sort it out and let me know. I'll be right next door." Sage waves at our shared wall.

Tess doesn't miss the point. "I can give you a ride any time you want or need a pick up."

Sage snorts and mouths "subtle" at me.

I chuckle and wave her off. "Weren't you leaving?"

"Yeah, yeah. Off to work I go." She whistles a few notes from Snow White. "Namaste."

Tess misses the sarcasm in Sage's voice.

"I'll stop by the shop sometime to say hi," Tess says as she pets my thigh. Between the ride comment and the leg petting, she's as subtle as an elephant.

Once the door closes, I fake a yawn by stretching and opening my mouth. "Oh, man. These pills are knocking me out."

Tess is still staring at my front door. "You two have a thing going on?"

She missed the best fake yawn ever. "No, we're friends."

"Friends with benefits?"

"If by benefits you mean muffins, then yes. If you're trying to politely ask me if I'm fucking my neighbor, then the answer is none of your business."

She twists to face me. "Sorry. The hippie yoga girl doesn't seem your type. I've watched you play on the field. So much passion and strength in one package."

I move her hand from getting anywhere near my package. "Sage teaches barre. She trained as a dancer. Have you seen a ballerina's feet? Talk about strength and passion."

She tips her head. "Remind me again why you won't sleep with me."

"Tess." My voice holds a cold warning. "I'm trying to be a gentleman here."

"I won't tell anyone."

Maybe she thinks I'm new to this game. I won't tell anyone. I'm on the pill, you don't need a condom. I won't share the picture.

"I'm sure you wouldn't, but secrets have a way of getting out."

Reluctant acceptance finally spreads across her face. With a nod, she stands. "Is Landon seeing anyone? Maybe you can introduce us."

Problem solved. "I'd be happy to."

Drew laughs when I tell him about my ankle. He's not without sympathy, but after fifteen years living in this area, he's seen or done it all.

"At least you waited until the start of the off-season to be an idiot. I should probably say thank you for your good timing. Give me a call the end of May. Maybe we can put you on a few shifts for Memorial Day weekend."

I thank him and hang up. A long month of no work, no training, nothing to do lies ahead of me. I'm not used to doing nothing. It's been two days and already I'm bored. No work and no play will make me a very dull boy.

Thanks to Tess, I've eaten more carbs and bread than I do in a month, except during rugby season. I pat my normally ripped stomach. Is that a new softness over the muscle? All I've done is nap and eat.

I know I need to keep off my ankle and have it elevated as much as possible for the first couple of weeks, but my doctor didn't say anything about not exercising.

I shuffle some things around in the living room until I can lie on the floor and prop my lower legs on the coffee table.

I'm in the middle of my third set of crunches when a key slides in the lock and the door opens.

"Someone's feeling better." Sage carries two canvas shopping bags into my kitchen.

I tilt my head back to watch her, but don't shift my position.

"You should put on a shirt. You're probably sweating on your rug."

"Pfft. I barely break a sweat with a few crunches. You can stay and watch if you don't believe me."

I return to doing ab work, twisting my torso to hit my obliques. When I turn to the left, I can see Sage watching me.

Her cheeks pink a little. "I brought you groceries. Meat, veggies, and that horrible protein powder you love."

"You're a lovely girl, sweet Sage."

She tucks a stray hair behind her ear. "Don't start being nice and thinking your flirting ways will work on me."

I sit up, letting my legs rest out in front of me. "Never. What are you going to cook for me?"

She makes my favorite face with scrunched up nose, pursed lips, and her eyes fighting amusement. It's supposed to be fierce. Like a kitten.

"Because I'm being sweet I thought I'd make a batch of my mother's beef stew. Hearty, full of iron and meaty goodness to heal bones."

"With little peas? My mum added them to her stews."

She lifts a bag of frozen peas from her "You're Kale-ing me, Smalls" bag. "Done."

I shuffle myself up onto one leg and hop over to my crutches. My shirt lies on the back of the chair where I threw it earlier.

I pull it over my head while balancing on one foot.

"Don't get dressed for me."

A snort escapes me. If only she were serious. "In that case . . ."

I reach for the waist of my pants. Underneath I'm wearing boxer briefs, but Sage doesn't know that.

She screeches when I thumb the fabric lower. "Stop! Nobody wants to see that!"

"Are you sure? I'll show you mine if you show me yours." I waggle my eyebrows at her.

"Stop your nonsense. We're not that kind of friends, Stan."

"Why do you always call me Stan? You and my father are the only two people who call me that except my granny who calls me Stanley."

"You're a Stan if I've ever met one. It suits you."

I tug down my T-shirt. "I prefer it when you call me Lee."

She opens the fridge and begins unpacking the groceries. "I'll stick with Stan the Man Bun."

I touch the knot of hair on my head. "The ladies love it."

"The ladies who love it are flattering your ego by lying to your face. You're an Instagram trend, my friend. A fad. The mullet of our generation."

"Ouch. I prefer to think of it as the sexy version of the stache from the seventies."

"Also not sexy on most men."

I hobble over on my crutches and rub my bun on her arm.

"Eww! It's like an extra hairy kiwi!" She runs to the opposite side of the island.

I pretend I'm going to chase her, but we both know she'll easily outrun my crutches.

"You should be resting, not harassing me with your fashion crisis."

With a sigh, I agree, "Fine. Want to watch a movie?"

"Let me start the stew and then we can hang out."

I prop myself up on the sofa with a view of her in my kitchen. She's at home here, chopping away. Garlic and onion go into the pot after she browns the meat. The aroma from the combination makes me homesick for my mum. I still need to call her.

In a few minutes, stew bubbles in a pot on my cooktop.

"What do you want to watch?" She curls up in one of my armchairs.

I wake up at the end of *Alien*, Sage's choice. I've missed all the good parts. The room is darker. My mouth waters from the scent of delicious stew simmering.

"Hey, sleepy-head." Sage stretches like a cat, pulling her arms out in front of her. "Hungry?"

"Starved." I need to take a piss. Pain throbs in my ankle when I set it on the floor. I flinch and exhale through my mouth.

"Side of pain pills with your stew?" She hands me my crutches.

I laugh, distracting myself from the discomfort. She's making a face either at my laughter or something else.

"What? Why are you making that face?"

She wrinkles her nose. "You could use a shower."

I'm about to tell her I smell like a man and how many women love the way I smell. I lift my arm to take an exaggerated sniff when my own stench punches me in the nose.

"Wow."

"I know. I didn't want to say anything because I'm not even sure you can shower, but I could smell you from the chair earlier."

"I think I've gone beyond sexy man musk to full-blown musk ox."

She nods and steps farther away. "Do you have any extra garbage bags? We can wrap your boot if you have tape."

"There's tape in the junk drawer."

After locating both, she tries to hand them to me before realizing I can't carry anything. "Lead the way and I'll follow."

I thump along ahead of her to my bedroom's en suite bathroom.

Our condos might be identical, but Sage has never been in my bedroom before. Seems odd having her in here where I'm naked. We've crossed a line in our friendship.

"I imagined more trophies and framed photos of yourself in your bedroom." Her voice is higher than normal and she giggles.

"You'd think that." I sweep my arm around the neat space with a few old ski posters on several walls and a vintage rugby jersey framed on another. "It became too crowded in here with all my accolades. I set up a shrine in the guest room. Feel free to go in there and light a candle while I shower."

"You're arrogant and vain enough I believe you."

I give her a serious look with raised eyebrows. "You wound me."

"Stan, your ego is in fine health. Now do you need my help wrapping your foot?"

I don't think she realizes that to tape the bag, I'm going to have to strip naked from the waist down first. I lean against the vanity and rest the crutches against the cabinet. "This isn't my first time with a cast or boot. I think I can handle it. Unless you want to see me naked."

Her mouth pops open. "I, I'm not. I didn't offer to scrub your back."

I pick up the plastic and tape. "I won't be able to bag the boot with my pants on. Or remove my boxers once everything is taped."

"Oh!" She plays with the small charm necklace at her throat. Color blooms on her chest beneath her hand. "I hadn't thought about that."

"Didn't think so." We're walking along a precipice here and I can see the rocks below us, ready to shred our friendship. "Now shoo."

With a squeak, she dashes out of the bathroom.

FOUR

SAGE

I BASICALLY OFFERED to wash Stan's back for him. Naked.

His naked back. Not me being naked. Although maybe that was implied. Or is it inferred? I can never keep those straight.

The point is, I followed him into his bedroom and basically stood there waiting for him to drop his pants.

Thankfully, he didn't, and I still have a small scrap of dignity to cling to.

Two days ago when he said his favorite color was pink and then stared at my pink hair, I'm certain my entire body turned the same shade.

He's not himself this week. It must be the pain and drugs. He's not working and is probably bored out of his mind. That explains all the weird things he's been saying.

I'm sure Tess would be in there right now with a soapy cloth, carefully cleaning every one of his parts, not standing in front of the door to his guest room, contemplating spying.

Is it snooping if he basically challenged me to look?

I open the door to find a neat office. A few trophies line the top of dark wood bookshelves on one wall. No modeling photos decorate the other walls. A few frames filled with what look like family pictures break up the rows of books. He has a lot of books.

This information surprises me. I know he went to university and has his degree in psychology, but he's a jock and a bartender. Not the most intellectual pursuits.

Geez, I sound like my father talking about dancing and teaching barre. His words "less than impressed" come to mind.

Down the hall, the sound of running water comes from Stan's bathroom. He's naked.

I need more distance. Like any normal person would in this situation, I run down the hall on my tiptoes and throw myself on the sofa.

As I catch my breath, I realize I've left the door open, basically broadcasting my snooping ways.

I dash to the office as his shower turns off. I don't want to be caught lingering around in the hall. I full out sprint to my spot and pull the blanket over myself.

My chest heaves with quick breaths. Before I see him, I hear the thumping of his crutches on the hardwood in his room.

I panic and reach for something to read to make it look like I haven't been acting like an untrustworthy weirdo left unsupervised in his house.

At least I didn't snoop through his drawers or steal his underwear.

I wonder if women steal his boxers as trophies. Or the long hairs from his fancy boar bristle brush I spotted in the bathroom. He has nicer grooming supplies than most women I know.

"Why are you so flushed and out of breath?" He's staring at me from the opening to the hall. "If I didn't know you better, I'd guess you were doing something naughty out here."

It's not fair how amazing he looks right out of the shower.

He's towel dried his hair so it's wavy and almost brushes his shoulders. A few lucky droplets of water darken his gray T-shirt. He's managed to dress himself in a fresh pair of lounge pants and a single thick sock covers his non-booted foot. He's supremely good looking, even damp.

I tend to favor a pink semi-drowned rat when wet. Pale hair, pale eyes, and pale skin make for a lovely pet rat.

"With the color on your cheeks, I'm beginning to think you really were up to no good. Did you watch a porno on my tele?"

We both glance at the black screen of the TV I haven't bothered to turn on.

"I see you found my latest copy of Rugby World. Anything catch your interest?"

I glance down at the magazine in my hand having no idea what it's doing there. "Um." Think of something interesting to say. "I didn't know there were so many types of fancy shoes."

Fascinating Woman of the Year award goes to Sage Blum, of the Chicago Blums. Her parents are so proud.

"I'll take your silence as acknowledgment of your guilt." He hops to the arm chair and settles in, resting his booted foot on the coffee table.

His clean scent, a mix of soap and shampoo waft over to me. "You smell much better."

He smiles, almost looking embarrassed as he picks a tiny bit of fluff off his dark gray pants. "Is the stew done?'

I forgot all about dinner. "You hungry?"

"Starving." His words come out a little sleepy and slurred.

By the time I've ladled stew into bowls, soft snoring comes from the chair.

Stan's snoring proves he's imperfect.

Leaving his bowl on the counter, I settle myself in the corner of the sofa. I flip on the TV but keep the volume low. I can't resist scrolling through his premium channels. Outlander is on demand. When Outlander is an option, the option is always Jamie Fraser.

Quietly eating, I rewatch one of my favorite episodes. Of course it's one with lots of naked Jamie.

For obvious reasons.

My spoon is halfway to my mouth with my last bite when I hear a chuckle from Stan during a particularly vigorous sex scene.

"Busted."

I drop my spoon, stew splattering off the side of the bowl and onto my chest. I wipe at it with my sleeve, only making the mess bigger. My cheeks heat when I catch Stan staring at me rubbing my chest. His attention and the friction causes my nipples to peak. I look down to confirm and cross my arms. "Hungry?"

He nods but doesn't look me in the eye. When I stand, his eyes track up my body. I quickly pad over to the kitchen and serve him a bowl.

Some barrier between us is thinning and disappearing. I wonder if he can feel it, too.

"Do you want toast or bread with your soup?"

"Sure. I'm not sure if I have any, but there might be crackers in the cupboard."

I open the cupboard to find three boxes of saltines and various other crackers. "You weren't kidding about your love for crackers."

"I will not be shamed." He shifts in his chair before standing and claiming my spot on the sofa where he can elevate his leg on the chaise.

He strokes his short beard around his lips. It's very distracting, so I know he must be doing it intentionally.

I've visited him at work a few times to watch him in action with his customers. The ladies love him. Gay men, too. Hell, anything with eyes and a pulse. He smiles, flirts, shakes his cocktails, and makes whoever he is focused on feel like they're the only person in the world who matters.

"Stop that." After setting his stew on the coffee table, I pick up my empty bowl.

"Stop what?"

"Turning on your charms."

He blinks a few times, looking confused and completely innocent. Until a slow, sly grin spreads along his mouth. "Are they working?"

Ignoring him, I turn to rinse out my bowl. I still have splatters on my shirt, so I dab a wet paper towel on the fabric.

"I think you're immune to my charms," Stan mumbles from his spot.

"I'm probably the only one. It's good for your ego. I keep you grounded." I say all this out loud while I'm thinking how not immune I am.

"You're good to me. This dinner is delicious."

I beam with pride over his simple compliment. "Thanks."

He's focused on shoveling bits of beef and vegetables into his mouth. He must not notice my wet shirt.

"Much better than the weird quinoa and chia seed thing you called pudding a few months back." His eyes flick over to me, then refocus on his bowl, almost like he's intentionally avoiding looking at my chest.

"It didn't have quinoa. Only chia seeds and almond milk."

"Still not a proper pudding. Someday I'll get my mother's recipe for Malva pudding and make it for you. Then you'll know South African pudding. Nothing can beat it."

He doesn't talk much about growing up in Cape Town or

anything to do with his family. I know his mother lives there. He's close with her. He never willingly discusses his father. It's easy enough to conclude they're not on the best terms.

"Get the recipe and I'll make some for you. You need comfort food."

"You'd make it for me?" A genuine, not flirty smile lights up his eyes. He looks like a kid on Christmas morning. "How about Hertzoggies?"

"I can try. Altitude might change things, but I can attempt it."

"Deal. Now tell me about this soft core porno you've been watching while I've innocently napped like a babe beside you."

"It's not porn! You really must think I'm a pervert with all of your porn references tonight."

"When I opened my eyes, there were naked people on screen having sex. I might have missed the beginning, but as far as I could see, none of the important bits were shown. Therefore, not full on porn, but soft core. Like on French television."

"It's a drama about time travel and eighteenth century Scotland."

"Ah."

"What?"

"Gotcha. It's intellectual. My apologies." He puts a big chunk of meat into his mouth and chews while watching me.

"You might enjoy it. Lots of naked breasts. Plus all the guy stuff."

"Aren't naked breasts guy stuff?"

"You know what I mean. Wars, fights, swords, espionage, and naked breasts."

"It sounds like James Bond in kilts."

"Better."

"Maybe I should watch from the beginning."

I nod. "We can start tonight if you're awake enough for it."

He fiddles with the remote and brings up the on demand feature. "Ready?"

I fluff his two lonely throw pillows and make myself comfortable on the other end of the sofa. "Do you need anything?"

"I'm good."

I've read all the books and seen the show repeatedly. I'm a little obsessed and can probably recite chunks of dialogue verbatim at this point.

Stan tosses half of the throw blanket over my legs.

I can feel his body warmth a few feet away. "This is better than Netflix and Chill."

"We should have our own tagline. Stew and Stare? Soup and Kilts?"

"Those are both terrible." I laugh at the idea of stew being part of a casual hookup.

"Demand and slurp?" He winks.

"Gross! Sounds like a bad date asking for a blow job."

His easy smile fades. "Has that happened to you before? A date demanding oral sex?"

I give him a sidelong glance, my mouth hanging open in disbelief. "Um, all guys?"

His head jerks back. "All guys do not do that. I've never done that."

"Probably because you don't have to. Women willingly and speedily offer to pleasure you all the time. Which is fine. I'm not judging your opportunities." I so am. "But in the real world where the rest of us live, most women don't drop to their knees and open their mouths with one look. Those women are often being paid for their enthusiasm."

"I've never asked, forced, or paid a woman to do anything she's not keen to do. Ever." His brows are lowered in a serious expression. I swear his eyes are a darker shade of pale, too.

"Perhaps you've always dated terrible men."

Neither of us say Logan's name again.

No need to repeat the conversation.

"It's different for us regular people."

"Define regular?"

I sweep my hand down my body. "Normal."

He leans over and tugs a strand of my hair. "There is nothing regular or normal about you, my pink-haired flower."

My hair's not the only thing pink now. My cheeks flush from his words or his proximity. Maybe both.

I point at the TV. "Focus on the wonder of Outlander, Mr. Sweet Talker."

"I wonder how I'd look in a kilt."

I'm never going to survive with an image of him wearing a kilt, and only a kilt, in my head.

"Terrible. Obviously, you have weak ankles."

"You've found my one weakness."

"I take solace in your imperfections. Now pay attention. This part's important."

He's snoring again by the middle of the second episode. I finish and quietly clean up without waking him before going home.

FIVE

STAN

MY CAR HAS been sitting outside for four days. A few inches of snow coat it and the driveway. I stare outside the living room window at both, thinking about the night spent watching movies with Sage.

I should move the Rover into the garage. Only I'm not supposed to drive. Parking isn't really driving. I can operate the pedals with my left foot.

I grab my keys and hold them in my mouth by the leather key fob. One issue solved. As I thump my way to the car, one crutch slips a little and I have to set my boot down harder than I'd like. I cringe, waiting for the pain to pass. When it does, I fumble with the keys and click the remote to unlock the door.

Getting into the Rover with a boot and crutches isn't as easy as I imagined when I concocted this adventure. Step close enough to open the door, then hop to the side to open it. Toss crutches inside and shove them into the passenger seat. Pivot and jump on one leg to get self into the driver's seat. Swing bad foot in first, follow by left foot. Adjust legs so left leg can reach the gas pedal. Curse.

With more cursing, I finally pretzel myself into position, and insert the key. Loud pinging sounds because the door is still open and the seatbelt isn't fastened. I hit the button to open the garage door.

Not smooth at all, but doable. I've got this.

With a glance down, I press the brake with my left foot and put the car in gear.

I ease off the brake and the Rover moves forward slightly. If the driveway weren't at a reverse incline, I might be able to coast into the garage. However, I don't have enough momentum to make it. I adjust my legs and attempt to press the gas with my left foot without knocking my boot.

The car lurches forward and I barely slam the brake to stop me from launching through the rear wall.

I don't die. The car isn't destroyed. I consider this outing a success all around.

After turning off the engine and disengaging myself, my boot, and the crutches, I step out of the car. Feeling proud, I give myself a mental high five.

Until I see Sage glaring at me from the open garage. "You're not supposed to be driving!"

"I wasn't. I was parking. Much different. Hardly any gas or steering needed." I give her a grin. "Aren't you proud of me?"

"No. You're a terrible patient. I told you I'd drive you anywhere you need to go."

"That's sweet of you, but I'm clearly able to manage."

"Hand over the keys." She opens and closes her right fist.

"You can't be serious." I get my crutches organized and walk over to her.

"I am. Give 'em up. You're not to be trusted." A small line creases her skin between her eyes.

I step as close as possible to her with my crutches. Even

slumped over, I tower above her. Typically I save the physical intimidation for the pitch, but I'm feeling playful. She wants to boss me around? Let's see her try.

She thumps me in the middle of my chest. In defense, I grab her hand, and she wiggles the keys out of my fingers. "Nice try, big guy."

I bop her on the nose. "You'll have to play chauffeur now. And I'm not riding in your old Jeep with the wind blowing in through the wobbly windows."

I can't move quick enough to avoid her finger flick on my arm. "It's not that bad. It's a classic."

Her wood-sided Jeep Wagoneer is older than she is.

"You could always call Tess." She smirky-grins at me. Even if it's a dig, she's adorable making it.

I tap my chin. "Excellent idea."

"She'd probably offer to give you a ride," she gives me an exaggerated wink, "on her pleasure bus."

I snort. Sage is adorable when she gets riled up about various women in town she perceives as a potential girlfriend for me. "She already has. More than once."

"Ew." She shakes her hair over her shoulder and makes a sour face. "Although I'm not surprised. She was practically begging you to eat her Danish right in front of me. That's never a good sign."

Laughing, I follow her out of the garage and over to her front door. "I think she meant the actual pastry."

"The only buns she wants to sink her teeth into are yours. And I'm not talking about this travesty." Sage reaches up to pat my bun.

"You're a bun sexist. For all of your peace and Namaste ways, you have a lot of pent up negative energy about my hair."

A year or two ago, the bun was hip and got me a lot of

extra work as the edgy, but outdoorsy pretty boy. Now every snowboarder and teenager from Ohio has a faux hawk or bun. I've been thinking about cutting it off, but I'm lazy and like I've said before, the ladies love it. Everyone but Sage.

Yet her opinion matters more than the rest combined.

"I'm thinking about cutting it off."

She stops in front of me and I don't have time to change my trajectory. I bump into her, dropping a crutch and grabbing her hip to stop us both from crashing to the ground.

Her hip is softer and fleshier than I would've imagined. I give it a squeeze before confirming with my eyes I'm not holding her hip.

I'm close, but a little farther back.

I'm holding her left cheek.

"Did you squeeze my ass?"

I'm still cupping it.

"That answers my question. Are you going to let go?" She hasn't jumped away.

God bless whoever invented yoga pants.

Reluctantly, I let go.

Sage takes a giant step away from me and my groping hand. Without meeting my eyes, she hands me back my crutch. An awkward silence blankets her living room like snow muffles all sound during a storm.

We don't do awkward. We joke and tease. Hang out. Other than the guys, she's my closest friend in Aspen.

Which means in my life. I need to say something to clear the fog.

"You've been working out."

Lame, but it makes her chuckle. "I had a class."

"I can tell."

"Was it the outfit?" She's wearing a tunic with the barre

studio's name across her chest. Her tank peeks through the sheer fabric.

"Of course." Until she mentioned it, I hadn't notice. "How's work?"

With a shrug, she walks into her kitchen. "Mostly regulars. I'm going to make a smoothie. You want one?"

"Will it have green things in it?"

"Probably." She opens the freezer and shakes a bag of frozen kale at me.

I squeak like a little girl. "Noo, not kale."

"You won't even taste it." She pulls out pineapple and frozen bananas, too.

With a glare, I make my way over to her counter stools at the island. The blender whirs with a concoction the color of grass.

"You drink that man-beast protein stuff, you can handle a little green smoothie." She pours a glass and sets it in front of me.

I sniff it. It mostly smells of pineapple. Mostly.

She gulps some of hers down and then smiles at me with a green mustache.

"That's not selling it. I'm not a rabbit."

"Try it. I'll owe you."

"A favor?"

"Within reason."

I narrow my eyes, inhale through my nose, and hold my breath as I take a sip. With my eyes closed, I can't tell I'm drinking salad.

It's not terrible. I fake a grimace. I'm excellent when it comes to faking emotions on my face thanks to years of modeling. "You owe me."

"Finish it and we have a deal."

"Tough girl." Closing my eyes, I chug the rest.

"What do you want in exchange?" Her voice sounds a little

nervous. "I've already committed to driving you around."

"After you confiscated my keys."

Her phone buzzes with a text. She reads it and frowns.

"Bad news?"

"Oh, it's nothing." Her voice drifts off as she types. "Family stuff back home."

After a few moments of furious texting, she sets down the phone. "So what's it going to be?"

"Huh?"

"The favor?"

I give her a slow, lopsided smile. "I'm going to hold onto this one for a while. I'll let you know when I'm ready to claim it."

"That wasn't part of the deal."

"You didn't mention a timeframe."

"Neither did you."

She scrunches up her face. "You don't play fair."

I laugh. "I always play fair. Ask anyone who's met me on a pitch. I play hard, I play smart, but never dirty. Unless there's mud involved."

"Will your favor involve mud?"

I answer with a small wink. "Can't say yet."

I have no idea what I'll ask for in return. I'm going to leverage a green smoothie into something bigger. That I know for sure.

SIX

SAGE

SOMEHOW I'M NOW beholden to Lee because of a green smoothie.

In terms of equal value, he's not crazy enough to ask for something big. A batch of cookies. A ride somewhere.

At least that's what I convince myself.

I don't handle being indebted well.

He's torturing me by not calling in his favor. It's been three weeks and still nothing.

I'm perpetually waiting for the other smelly size twelve rugby shoe to drop.

At the shop, I'm folding lacy underwear when the chimes ring above the door.

Cheeks is a tiny boutique tucked off the Hyman Street pedestrian mall in the center of Aspen. I know. Hyman is a homonym for hymen. The irony.

Surrounded by brick buildings dating from the silver mining era of the town, our white painted wood trim and small hanging sign stand out if anyone peeks down the alley.

Owned by the coolest woman I've ever met, Cheeks is an elegant and unique lingerie shop. Customers return season after season, year after year. We carry brands from Europe not stocked anywhere else in the state.

In general, I love our clients. Occasionally we'll get a creep who asks rude questions or requests us to model something. Typically we laugh off such requests and coolly send them on their way. We've never needed a security guard, and honestly, I don't know where one would fit in our tiny space.

"Hi, Sage," a familiar voice greets me.

Tess stands on the threshold, a sly smile on her face. At least she's not showing me her teeth. I plaster on a smile and greet her, "Oh, hi, Tess."

"I adore this shop." Her eyes widen in forced enthusiasm. Fake lashes make her peepers extra-large.

The better to judge you with, my dear.

I've never seen her in her before. That doesn't mean she doesn't shop here, but the timing is odd given I met her a few weeks ago at Stan's.

"You must spend your entire paycheck on pretty things in here." She strokes a pale rose silk kimono edged in delicate black lace hanging near the door.

"I have the underwear collection of a courtesan." I don't know why I feel the urge to bait her. Most of my "lingerie" comes from the organic cotton selection we hide in the corner. I'm not saying I wear granny panties, but lace shows under yoga shorts and pants. I do have a few nice things bought on sale and with my steep employee discount. Those pieces are still tucked in tissue in one of my drawers.

Tess's eyes sparkle. She's moved onto the toys. "What do you recommend? As one single girl to another?"

Ignoring her dig at my implied lack of sex life, I meet her at the glass case near the register.

"They're the best. Velvety soft silicone. Totally worth the price." Our "pleasure enhancers" are discreet and more expensive than typical brands. I pull out the most expensive vibrator and make sure the price tag is visible when I set it on the glass.

This time when Tess's eyes widen, it's in shock. "That's a lot of money to get off."

"It is, but it will always work. Can't say that about a date, no matter how expensive the meal or drinks." I give her a conspiratorial wink like we're friends.

We're not.

"I bet you get a lot of men in here buying gifts for their girlfriends and wives."

"Sometimes they buy for both. We try not to judge."

Thoughts of being a kept woman light up her face. "They're so lucky."

I'm not sure if she means the men or the girlfriends. She can't possibly mean the wives. I set the silicone toy back in the case. "Anything else I can help you with?"

Her gaze flicks to the clearance rack before she taps her pointy nails on the glass.

The better to claw out your eyes with, my dear.

"As a matter of fact, yes. I wanted to chat with you about our mutual friend."

My mind blanks on who we know in common. Other than Lee.

Ignoring my silence, she starts talking again. "He said the two of you are friends, so I thought maybe you could give me some tips on getting to know him better. What he likes. Dislikes. Favorite foods. That sort of thing."

I still have no clue who she's babbling about. With a silent prayer, I ask, "Who?"

She tucks her chin and bats her lashes at me. "Starts with an L."

Ohdeargodno. She's not really here to pick my brain about Lee.

I remain mute and return to straightening the shop.

"I'm sorry if it's a touchy subject. I didn't know you two had a dating past."

"We don't. We're neighbors and friends."

"Landon lives in the same condo complex? Wow. You're a lucky girl with all that man candy a few feet away at all times."

"What? No. Landon lives with Easley in Basalt."

"Then why did you call him your neighbor?"

"I didn't. Lee is my neighbor."

She gives me a look that says she thinks I'm crazy. "I know that. I was there. In his condo. Remember?"

This entire conversation is an infinite loop of confusion.

"You said our mutual friend and the name begins with L."

"I meant Landon. Landon Roberts? I assumed since you hang out with all the rugby players, you were friends with him, too."

I exhale in relief. "Oh, Landon with an L."

"How else do you spell Landon?"

"I thought you meant Stanley."

Nothing.

"The old guy who always makes the cameos in The Avengers movies?"

Oversimplified, but still correct. "No, not the Marvel Comics' legend, who doesn't live in Aspen as far as I know. Lee. My neighbor."

I expect smoke to come out of her ears as she tries to unravel this conversation.

"For some reason, Lee's not interested in me. Something

about working together and non-fraternity clauses. Landon being his teammate seems like a good second choice. Plus, he doesn't work at the same resort."

I snicker and try to make it sound like a sneeze by adding "choo" to the end.

"Bless you."

"Thanks."

"So? Do you know Landon well?"

Too well. "Not really, but we did go out for a short while."

Not short enough.

"I thought so by your reaction earlier. I could tell you had feelings for him."

I laugh. "I really don't. You should totally go out with him. The rugby guys usually hang out at Little Annie's for happy hour on Wednesdays. Or anytime there's a major match on TV."

"You should come along. You know all of them and can introduce me!"

Is she asking me to be her wing-woman? Doesn't she have a collective of like-minded harpies she can hang out with?

"A bunch of us can go together."

That's subtle. With Stan on the sidelines with his ankle, there is no way I'm going to troll the players while they're drinking and getting rowdy.

SEVEN

SAGE

"PARSLEY, SAGE, ROSEMARY, and Thyme!" Easley yells from the back of the bar at Little Annie's.

"Easley," I mumble and narrow my eyes. Clearly, I have zero backbone and can't lie. Tess stopped by work as I was closing to drag me here. I couldn't even come up with a plausible excuse. Telling her a flat out no seemed rude. I may not like her, but I don't want her for an enemy either. Aspen's too small of a town for girl gangs.

Easley drapes his giant gorilla paw over my shoulder, pulling me into a hairy one-armed hug and crushing my face into his ribs. Not only is he dark and furry, he's more mountain than man. Unlike the true rugby fangirls, I can never keep the positions straight. I'm pretty sure Easley's a forward. Stan's a back because he's very fast.

Easley's face resembles the Thing from Fantastic Four. I'm sure his nose has been broken more than once and his forehead ridge makes him look like he drags women back to his cave.

Despite having the foulest mouth and picking fights, he's a nice enough guy. I suppose.

Other than singing the same silly song lyrics every time he sees me, that is.

I grumble about not being part of an herbal girl band, but no one can hear me above the roars over something happening on the bar's multiple televisions.

Because I'm here to introduce Tess and her girlfriends to the guys, I look behind me to get it over with. No one is standing between me and the door I came through less than twenty-seconds ago. I scan the room for Tess.

Speaking of fast . . .

Tess and her two friends are squeezed in between Landon and some other guy at the bar. Her friends are pretty. Of course.

I check my texts to see if Zoe has responded. I have one from her telling me she has evening clients and won't be done until nine. Too late for happy hour and I'm not sure how long I'm going to last out on a Wednesday night with the league of numskulls.

The friend whose name I think is Kelsie, or something that rhymes with Kelsie, waves me over to join them. Compared to the other two women, she doesn't fit their look. A little curvier than me, her hair is a few shades darker blond. She's not wearing a ton of makeup and can probably breathe in her jeans. Other than questionable taste in friends, she seems the coolest of the three.

There's not enough room to squeeze between the guys and the bar. I stand a few feet away, watching the mating dance begin.

Tess giggles loudly, points over to me, and then sticks her hand out for Landon to shake. He follows her finger and gives me a wide, cautious grin before gripping her hand, bringing it up to his mouth, and kissing her knuckles.

So gallant and so gross.

I can't believe I slept with him. Beefcake blonds aren't my type. The circumference of his thigh is larger than his IQ.

Easley looms over me. "Shouldn't you be at home taking care of our boy wearing a sexy nurse costume?"

"Lee's costume doesn't fit me. I was going to ask to borrow yours, but I'm afraid it might be too big."

It takes a few beats for my joke to click and he laughs. "Nah, why'd you think I'd have any sort of lady costumes laying around my place?"

"Maybe because you always dress in drag for the end of season shenanigans on the mountains? I'm not judging, by the way. I love that you're comfortable enough in your skin to explore your feminine side."

The esteemed members of the Pitkin Rugby Club have an annual tradition involving hideous cocktail dresses, an unfortunate amount of blue eye shadow and red lipstick, and a howling run down Ajax the last week of ski season. It all begins and ends with too many cocktails, more than one person jumping into the pool at Little Nell, and sworn oaths to never post any photos online.

A month ago, Stan wore a lovely off the shoulder red dress with sequin accents and a tulle skirt. With his dark hair in a twist, he was by far the prettiest boy in a dress, even with his beard. I'm tempted to pull up the pics on my phone.

"Oy. I didn't keep the dress. Not after it went in the pool and got mud on it." Easley makes a terrible woman with his hairy chest and broad shoulders.

"Sure. You didn't have it dry cleaned for later?"

He pauses. "I hadn't thought of that. Damn."

I can't tell if he's serious or teasing. I decide on serious. It's more fun.

Loud giggling from the bar causes us both to look.

"Friends of yours?" he asks, eyeing the woman vying with Tess for Landon's attention.

"No, not really. The brunette in the middle is a friend of Lee's. I think she has the hots for Landon."

"She seems friendly." As we stare, Tess gets close enough to Landon; she's practically dry humping him.

"Very."

"Are the others single? I think the brunette one on the left is a massage therapist at the Ritz." He drops his arm from its resting place on my shoulder. "Can you introduce me?"

I dramatically place my hand over my heart. "You wound me, Ryan Easley."

He ruffles my hair with a chuckle. "Sorry, sweetheart. You're officially off limits."

I arch an eyebrow. "There's an official off-limits list at the club? Is it laminated?"

He lowers his deep brows. "You're not supposed to know that. Is Barnyard sharing our secrets?"

Whoa. "I was kidding."

He straightens and rolls his thick neck. "Uh, yeah. So was I."

I squint up at him, attempting to decipher if he's stoned or not. "Okay. Sure. Let's go meet the girls."

Pushing him ahead of me, I use him as a plow to cut through the crowd.

Tess is too busy breathing on Landon to notice our arrival at the bar. So much for being new besties.

Kelsie and her rhyming friend grin at us . . . well, at Easley. I'm overshadowed by the big galumph.

"Ladies, have you met Ryan Easley yet? He's a rugby player, too. In case you couldn't tell." Or are blind.

"I'm Chelsea," the curvy masseuse introduces herself.

Totally rhymes with Kelsie.

"Do you work at the spa at the Ritz?" Easley asks like the stalker he is.

She smiles. "I do. How'd you know that?"

Color darkens his pale cheeks.

"I told Ryan I thought you looked familiar when we met." I cover for him because I don't really think he's a stalker. It's a small world for us worker bees. I suppose we're townies.

The thought makes me smile. My mother would be appalled.

Soon Easley and Chelsea are head-to-head talking about sports massages. Kelsie sips her drink through her tiny cocktail straws. Our gazes catch.

Then there were two.

I lean closer. Since my role here is to play matchmaker and not hook-up, I can at least find someone for her to chat up.

"Anyone catch your eye?" My smile is friendly and conspiratorial.

She nods and takes another long sip of her drink. "He just walked in."

I twist to scan the room, but her hand on my arm stops me. "Don't look. He's coming to the bar."

I nod, wishing I had eyes in the back of my head. Behind me, a couple of guys greet the newcomer with loud backslaps and enthusiastic hellos. He must be a rugby player.

Kelsie sits up straighter on her stool and brushes her fingers through her hair. "Do I look okay? Anything in my teeth?"

I examine her smile for stray seeds or greens. "Nope. You're good. He must be cute."

"He's the most gorgeous man ever. I've had a crush on him since the first time I saw his poster." She adjusts her top to reveal more cleavage.

"Huh?" Before I can get clarification, I catch a familiar voice in the crowd. I spin around. "Oh."

"Oh my rugby god is more like it. Or the Big O." Kelsie's humor makes me smile. We could be friends if she weren't crushing on Stan.

"Isn't the man bun a little ridiculous? He probably has a tiny penis and is trying to compensate with longer hair."

"You're hysterical. I've seen him play rugby. Those shorts don't hide much. Even without the details, a tiny penis wouldn't have that kind of bounce."

My eyebrows climb almost to the top of my head. "Um, wow. You really pay attention."

"There's a Tumblr page for all the PRC guys. You should check it out. Helps make those long winter nights pass. If you know what I mean."

I do. I do know what she means. "How did I miss that?"

She pulls out her phone and taps away for a moment. "This is a great shot. Gives you an idea of the full kit and the caboodle."

I take the phone from her. On the screen is a pic of Stan from last year's fall rugby fest. He's sweaty and full out running with his shirt slightly lifted, exposing his happy trail over tight abs. There is a certain tenting going on in the front of his shorts.

"Zoom in," Kelsie encourages.

I do.

No way to pretend I'm not staring at Stan's junk.

"What's so fascinating, ladies?" the man himself asks.

I bobble and nearly drop the phone, but Stan's hand reaches out and saves it from certain cracked-screen death on the floor.

"Someone's a club fan." He stares at the picture.

I grab for it. "Kelsie and I were discussing . . ." My mind goes blank.

Kelsie pipes up, "The uniforms. I was saying that I think the shorts are longer this year. Did you make a change to them?"

I want to high five her, but that would be too obvious.

Instead I give her a subtle thumb's up.

Unfortunately, we're too distracted by being proud over our cover-up; we fail to retrieve her phone before Stan can adjust the photo.

"Well, this is interesting." He needlessly shows us the screen. As if we don't know what we were looking at. His grin reaches his eyes and the corners crinkle with his delight at catching us. "PRiCks. Clever name."

I want a hatch to open below my feet and swallow me. Or a vortex to appear between us and suck me into another dimension.

Finally doing something I should've done before he ever saw the screen, I snatch the phone from him and toss it to Kelsie. "Kelsie, meet Stan. Lee. Meet Lee."

"The comic book guy?"

"Afraid I'm not that clever. No, just Lee. Only Sage and my gran call me Stan."

"That rhymes," Kelsie purrs at him like he's the first man to string two words together.

"Nice to meet you, Kelsie. You're a friend of Sage's, then?" Stan slips into charmer mode.

"We only met tonight. I live in the same complex as Tess."

I see Stan's smile falter for a second before he recovers. "Ah, so you're neighbors like Sage and me."

Kelsie gives me a smile that feels more beauty queen than genuine. Our camaraderie from a few minutes ago fades as she realizes I'm in close proximity to her prize. "I didn't know that. How nice for you, Sage."

My name is a dried bunch of leaves on her tongue. No more girl bonding over the hot guy. I'm competition.

Honestly, I'm so tired of women always viewing each other as competitors. We're not in high school anymore, but it's still a contest to see who is most popular, has the prettiest eyes, or the cutest clothes. Hell no to the cutest couple being the hottest jock and the weird hippie girl who wears overalls and uses Kool Aid on her hair.

Not that Stan and I are a couple. Apparently, I'm on every rugby players' no fly list. Lucky me. I need to talk to him about that. I mean the Landon thing ended badly, and I have recently sworn off any and all men who have any athletic skills, but it's my choice. Not a bunch of testosterone fueled short-wearing, penis-bouncing cavemen with Easley, their Neanderthal King.

"You should sit down." Kelsie offers Stan her stool while pulling me out of the way. "Are you okay?"

"Yeah, are you okay? Are you even allowed to be out and about?" I poke his shoulder when he passes me. "Wait, you didn't drive yourself here, did you?"

"Calm down. I rang Darren and he gave me a lift. If you'd ever check your phone, Miss Chauffeur, I wouldn't have had to rely on others." He leans his crutches against the bar and hops on the stool.

I stick my tongue out at him. It's extremely immature and satisfying. He responds with the same, which cracks me up. Kelsie observes us with crossed arms. I'm not sure if she's doing it intentionally to emphasize her ample chest, but it's working.

"Check your phone," Stan says.

Indulging him, I search my bag and find it. With a tap of the screen I see five text messages and two missed calls from him.

"Oops." I start reading the texts. "I should've realized you'd want to come to the weekly gathering of the brain trust. I'm sorry I didn't think to swing home and pick you up. Tess showed up and we came straight here."

"It's all right. I'm surprised you came without me. You normally complain all the way here and then all the way home about the stench of too many rugby gorillas in an enclosed space."

"Who are you calling a gorilla?" Easley's furry arm wraps around my shoulders again. The hairs on his forearm tickle my neck, making me shiver.

"Have you heard of PRiCks?" Stan asks.

"Oh, yeah. It's all pics of the player's junk." Easley sounds too proud of this fact. "Quite a few of yours truly. Naturally. You've never seen it?"

Stan stares at me.

I stare back.

He fake coughs. "How very interesting. Sage and Kelsie were showing it to me a few minutes ago."

Easley snorts. "It's a pity Sage is on the list."

Stan focuses over my shoulder, his eyes flashing with annoyance and something territorial. "We're not supposed to talk about that."

I try to lift Easley's arm. "Too late. He told me earlier. Why am I on some sort of don't touch, don't tell list?"

Stan does that guy thing where he fills his cheeks with air and then blows out a big breath. "Honestly? After Landon?"

I finally free myself from the gorilla grip. "One bad apple."

"You've sworn off all rugby players and men who get regular exercise. What does it matter?" He rolls up the cuff of his button down, momentarily distracting me from coherent thoughts while I stare at his forearm and the glimpse of his tattoo.

"I don't need you protecting me. I'm not your little sister." Anger comes out of nowhere and seeps into my voice.

"No need to remind me," he mumbles and brushes a stray lock that's escaped the bun out of his eyes.

"Do you want a drink?" Kelsie hasn't given up.

"I'll take a club soda and lime."

"Nothing stronger?" She touches his arm.

"Not for me as long as I'm on my meds." He lifts the boot. An injured athlete is honey for the bears. Or pollen for the bees. I'm not sure which one is a better analogy.

Both Kelsie and Chelsea coo over Stan. Unless Easley begins spontaneously bleeding or stabs himself, he's lost the face-off.

"Want me to pretend to give you the Heimlich to get their attention back?" I happily offer.

"Nah. I already got Chelsea's digits. Let Lee have some attention. He's been stuck at home and sulking over the season."

He makes a good point. "How bummed is he about probably missing the start?"

"He's not getting any younger. Professional play isn't going to happen at this point, so any time he's not playing, it's one game closer to the end of his semi-pro career."

"The old guys at the club still play one or two tournaments a year."

"Have you ever seen one of those forty year olds the day after a match? Hobbling around with heat and ice, moaning about their joints?"

"Stan's not forty. He's a perfect specimen of athletic performance."

"At twenty-seven. You should find footage of him playing in his early twenties. You think he's fast now? He should've gone pro."

"Why didn't he?"

"My opinion and mine alone, he wanted to piss off his father."

"Stanley?" I barely know about the man other than he shares a name with his son and is madly ambitious.

"The man, the arsehole."

"He sounds like a winner."

"You've never met him?"

I shake my head. "How would I?"

"He comes through Aspen at least once a ski season for business meetings."

"Huh." Stan's never mentioned his father's visits. Then again, I don't exactly invite him over when my own parents visit. And neither of them is openly an arsehole.

"What are you two whispering about?" Stan pokes my shoulder with the end of his crutch. "Sharing secrets?"

"Easley was trying to convince me you stuff your shorts." Both men choke.

"No, I wasn't." Easley holds up his hands in innocence.

"You would know." Stan jokes. "No man can go through that many tube socks in as short of time as you do."

"I have pointy toes. They wear through the socks quicker than normal."

"Or it's your man sweat." I add to their good-natured teasing.

"Fine, if you must know, we were chatting about your daddy issues," Ryan says.

Whoa. Elbowing Easley, I whisper out of the side of my mouth. "Shh."

"Really?" Stan's expression turns cold. His eyes look even paler.

"No, not really." Given his icy posture, it's better to lie to my best friend than admit to gossiping about his family. "Why would we talk about your boring old family? Pfft."

I grin at him, hoping it will brighten his mood. This is the reason we never chat about family stuff. He shuts down. I can almost see the locks closing and keys turning behind his eyes.

Kelsie, immune to the silent struggle going on in front of her, chats away about summer plans. She rattles off activities like she's on the tourism board.

Turns out she is. Her job for the city involves tracking every single activity, be it a 5K for skin cancer or the farmer's market schedule.

Explains the bubbly personality and friendliness.

Summer in the mountains is my favorite. Everyone thinks of Aspen in the winter with the celebrities and winter sports. It's all glamour, fur and Kardashians. Summer is different. Long days, green Aspen trees, golden meadows . . . glorious. Skis give way to mountain bikes and hiking boots replace snowshoes. Horse rides take over from the dog sleds. Everyone seems mellower in the summer.

The dancers will return in a few weeks. I've signed up to be an assistant teacher for the teen program. Putting my dance major to work should please my own grumpy father. Even if it's for a few weeks a year.

"I can also get us tickets to the music tent at a discount." Kelsie is still talking. "If you like music."

I want to like her. I can always use more friends, girlfriends specifically. Stan doesn't count. For the obvious reasons posted on Tumblr and seared into my mind.

Unlike Tess, I can see hanging out with Kelsie. Unless she dates Stan. Not sure I could handle that.

Tess waves at me. "Landon and I are going to get a bite to eat at Mezza Luna."

I wait for the offer to join them. Thankfully, none follows.

"Enjoy!" I wave back with too much enthusiasm.

Stan lowers my arm for me. "You're welcome."

"For what?"

"I set that in motion." His hand rests on my bicep, creating a warm tingle on my skin.

"No you didn't. I'm the one who brought her here for the sole purpose of throwing her under the Landon bus."

"Who do you think suggested Landon might be interested in the first place?"

"Ooh, we're an evil duo." I hold up my hand for a high five. "Don't leave me hanging."

He slaps my hand and then weaves our fingers together. A small battle of wills ensues. I know I'll lose or he'll let me win, but I still try to best him. It's like freestyle arm wrestling with no leverage.

With a twist, he spins me around. I still refuse to let go or give up. My hand is over my head, exposing my ribs.

Bad move. I've left myself vulnerable to a side attack.

Stan tickles my ribs, keeping my right arm lifted with his left hand. Squealing, I attempt to squirm my way out of his torturous grip. I could use my free elbow, but the man is injured. Something he's probably using to his advantage like a predator pretending to have a hurt paw. I'm not fooled.

When his hand brushes against the side of my breast, we both freeze.

EIGHT

STAN

MY FINGERS REST against the soft curve of Sage's breast.

I'm copping a feel of my best friend in a crowd of my rugby mates in the middle of happy hour at Little Annie's.

I can't jump away between my lame leg and the fact I'm seated on a stool. Instead, I freeze.

With my fingers still pressing into soft, warm Sage. Loud conversations continue around us over the noise from the televisions and background music.

Even if I weren't in the middle of a mini-dry spell, my body would be reacting.

Right now every synapse fires like I'm a twelve-year-old boy again.

This is it, fellas.

What we've been waiting for!

Boob.

We're touching an actual bonafide girl boob.

I shake away the squeaky voice of my younger self and remove my hand from her chest.

This must snap the spell because Sage spins around. Her eyes are wide and her cheeks flush with deep rose. Her panting could be from the tickling and arm wrestling. Or the breast fondling.

Our hands are still linked together. I reluctantly release hers and let my hand drop to my lap. Thankfully I'm not twelve and tenting my shorts, but my blood flow has definitely shifted south from our not so innocent play.

"You don't play fair."

If she thinks that was a tactic to win, I'm relieved. "It was an accident."

In this light her eye color shifts to dark gray, but I know they're blue. Deeper than mine, hers remind me of the sky right before a storm. Vaguely green, sometimes gray, they're as unpredictable as the woman they belong to.

"Hmmph."

"Hmmph." I echo her as we continue to stare down each other. I've got all the time in the world.

It's been weeks and I'm cabin crazy. Not practicing, not working, and sitting at home stewing make my life boring as fuck.

When I walked into Annie's, I didn't expect to find Sage in the middle of the mutt pack, shining like a bright light in the dim bar, surrounded by big rugby players and women trying too hard to impress them. She and another blonde woman were chatting and laughing over something on their phone. Undetected, I could watch her without her making a stink about staring or asking if she had something on her face.

When I snooped over her shoulder, I never imagined she'd be looking at a pic of my shorts. From the way the image was enlarged, my shorts weren't the intended focal point of their discussion. No, what lies beneath held their attention.

Whoever thinks girls aren't as pervy as men is entirely misled. They're more perverted than us. By far. When I was thirteen, I made the mistake of picking up one of mum's romance novels during a holiday at the beach. After recovering from my shock, I snuck it into bed with me and read with a flashlight for most of the night.

I learned a lot.

My vocabulary increased tenfold.

Some things I wish I could erase.

"You blinked! I win!" Sage twists my shirtsleeve between her fingers.

"Whatever." I shrug, hiding my grin by twisting my lips to the side and running my hand over my shaggy beard.

Our awkward moment seems to be passing.

"You're looking a little crazy duck hunter and less super-modely metrosexual these days. You need a trim." Her hand pulls on the longer hairs on my chin.

"You could do it for me."

"You'd trust me with trimmers? I might go wild and decapitate your bun."

"I trust you." Implicitly. Sage and my mum. It's a short list.

"You shouldn't." She makes a scissor cutting motion. "In fact, you should probably make me give back my key. Better, change the locks."

I pull the elastic from my hair and hand it to her. "Happy?"

"I'm happier." Kelsie returns to my side and runs her fingers through my hair. I feel like a dog being petted by a stranger. I duck my head away from her hand and her ring gets caught in a knot.

"Ouch." Tilting my head to release the tension, I use my fingers to extract her hand.

"Not into hair pulling?" she purrs. "Isn't that why all guys have long hair? Something for women to hold onto and pull? Or even better, steer?"

Sage snorts from beside me.

My eyes widen to the size of frisbees.

"Steering!" Sage gives Kelsie a high five. "That's brilliant!"

"You've never done that? It's kind of like riding a horse. Tug and he goes a little to the left." Both slip into a fit of giggles.

At my expense.

The poor, hopeless, injured boy who merely wants to hang out with his friends.

I pout and reclaim the hairband from Sage. I could do a ponytail, but no, she's getting full top of the head bun action. That'll serve her and her snark.

Holding the elastic between my teeth, I use both hands to put my hair on the top of my head.

"Wow. That's really sexy." Kelsie fans herself while Sage scowls.

"See? The ladies love it." I smirk and pat my head.

"Ridiculous with a capital ugly."

"I love it." Kelsie challenges Sage's snark.

If she weren't so handsy and forward, she'd be cool.

Sage rolls her eyes like the teenage girl she's mimicking. "On that note, I'm outta here. Stan, you want a ride?"

I wait for Kelsie to make the same double-entendre Tess said about Stan rides, but blessedly she doesn't. "Sure. All this vertical action has worn me out."

Kelsie's mouth twitches. I admit I lobbed that one to her.

"Come on, Romeo, let's get you home and put you to bed," Sage says.

Kelsie's eyes widen before she gives me a knowing little wink. "Must be nice to have a benefit plan with your neighbor. Lucky girl."

Sage ignores her or doesn't hear the comment.

I'm about to correct her misconception about my

relationship with Sage, but decide against it. Maybe if women think I'm taken, they'll ease off a little.

A plan hatches in my head. Sage dating me would also piss of Landon. I don't give a rat's ass what his opinion of me is, but it would be nice to rub it in his face that he had a woman like Sage and fucked it up.

"Remember the green smoothie bet?" I ask once we're in her Jeep.

"I remember a questionable bargain was made, but I wouldn't call it a bet. Why?"

"You should've been a lawyer. You're excellent at semantics."

"And you sound like my father."

"Smart and handsome?"

"A broken record of disappointment and judgment." Her frown is genuine.

How anyone could be disappointed in Sage blows my mind.

"In any case, I have an idea."

"Why does this worry me?" she asks.

"It's a mutually beneficial suggestion."

"Kind of like two kids on a playground offering to show each other their private parts?"

I choke on nothing. "Is that an option? You were looking at mine earlier on that girl's phone. You have me at a disadvantage."

"And you took a gander down my top when you were stoned on pain pills after the ER."

Guess I wasn't as subtle as I thought. I have a vague memory of small breasts with pert nipples. Unfortunately, like everything else from that night and weekend, the details are fuzzy. "I did not."

"Oh, you did. I forgave you because you were highly

medicated and not thinking straight."

"Gracious of you."

"Let's never speak of the Tumblr account again, m'kay?" She focuses on the traffic light in front of us.

"There's a Tumblr account only of me?"

"Ego, ego. You have to share the PRiCks love with all the guys on the team. Kelsie has a particular interest in yours. In case that wasn't obvious back there."

"American women have a reputation for being forward. Rightly so."

"Hey. Way to stereotype." She takes the left turn a little too fast and I shift into the door.

"You're also known as being bossy." I give her a slow smile. "And loose."

"Loose as in immoral or loose as in American vaginas are like everything else in this country, super-sized?"

Laughter bellows out of me. "Now there's something I never imagined coming out of your beautiful mouth."

She giggles. "I thought it was pretty funny. Not giant, loose vaginas. Those aren't funny. Kind of sad. Probably. I'm not saying I'm familiar with this issue. Bodies stretch and change from babies. Especially those super-size newborns with their enormous noggins."

I rest my head against the passenger window and listen to her babble. "Are you done?"

"It's a real issue for moms." She sounds sympathetic. "Rose shares all sorts of stories from her prenatal classes."

"When's the baby due?" I've only seen pics of Sage's older sister. They have the same eyes, but Rose is shorter and curvier. She lacks Sage's sparkle even though they're clearly sisters.

"End of July. I told her I appreciate her timing her procreation to coincide with the end of summer season here. She's very thoughtful that way."

"Will you go back for the birth?"

"I wouldn't miss it. I can't wait to meet my niece."

Like so many of our conversations, we've sidetracked from my intended topic into something unexpected and random. "I was saying . . ."

She gives me a quick glance out of the corner of her eye. "Sorry."

"I have a mutually beneficial proposition." My smile is lopsided and intentionally so.

"Okay?" Her voice softens to a whisper.

"We should let people assume we're a couple."

"Why would they think we're a couple?"

"We're always together and bicker constantly."

"I can see your point, but why?" Her gaze flicks to mine before returning to the road.

"Gives me a little breathing space from the smothering types who want to play nurse."

She giggles. "Easley asked why I wasn't home nursing you. It was weird and I think he was imagining me in a sexy nurse costume."

"Fucking Easley."

"He proves your point about people, or at least the rugby dogs, assuming we've got a thing going on." She waggles her eyebrows like a dirty old man.

"Let's exploit their assumptions. Plus, it will bug the shit out of Landon. He thinks he's a major stud."

Her snort is both loud and very un-ladylike. "False advertising."

I resist commenting because I really don't want to know anything about their sex life together. Ever. Sage is full of passion and unbridled spirit. Landon is bland from his blond hair to his personality. He also has the tiniest sausage fingers I've ever seen on a ruby player. Or any man.

Great. Now I'm thinking about the two of them having sex.

"Landon sees himself as my rival. It could be amusing to put him on his tiny stool in the naughty corner of the nursery school."

"Are you threatened by him?"

"No, but his annoying ways shouldn't go unpunished. It would be unsportsmanlike to take out one of my own players on the pitch. I'd probably be kicked out of the club. He's not worth the risk."

She presses her lips into a thin line.

"What?"

"I'm not a pawn in your male pissing contest, am I? Easley told me about some list at the club that I'm on."

The damn list. Every year we put names on pieces of paper of women who are off-limits for anyone in the club to date or fuck. Typically, it's birds we're chasing or involved with.

"It's a list of women in town who are untouchable. Everyone respects it."

"Why am I on it? Did Landon add me as some sort of crazy ex-girlfriend to be avoided?"

"I added you. Rugby players are all horny arseholes." After Landon screwed over Sage, I listed her. Technically, this means she's off limits to me, too. At least until after the big rugby fest that ends our year in September. I'm willing to break my own dating rules to prove a point to her and my teammates, although I'm not one-hundred-percent sure what the point is.

"Present company included?"

I'd stuffed myself into a corner with that comment. "No comment. You're not supposed to know the list even exists. Damn Easley and his big mouth. Take it as a compliment.

You're too good for those lumbering trolls."

"Again, I ask, present company included?" Her smile returns. A wicked gleam sparkles in her eyes.

"Unless you're calling me a troll, then yes. When have I ever not been a gentleman with you?"

"There was the shower incident recently."

"My memory is you ran away before any indecency could take place."

Her cheeks flush the same color as her hair.

"Let me think about this idea of yours. I'm sure it will all seem preposterous in the clear light of morning."

"I doubt that. It's a win-win. No money down. Zero risk opportunity." I thicken my accent, sounding like a South African infomercial host. "What do you have to lose?"

"My freedom?"

"Freedom is a false concept. Remember the green smoothie?"

"My kingdom for a kale smoothie. What was I thinking?"

"It'll be fun. You already hang out with me on a regular basis. You're my chauffeur of choice. You're stuck driving me around for a few more weeks at least."

I can tell I have her almost convinced when she pulls into her driveway next to mine. Out of time, I make her promise to think about it overnight. I gracefully extract myself from the Wrangler and hop to my door, a spring in my crutch-aided step.

"It'll be fun!" I shout at her as she walks to her own door.

"That's what Napoleon said right before marching his troops into Russia in the winter." Sarcasm colors her words.

"I prefer to think of this as Hannibal in the Alps with elephants. Elephants always equal a good time."

"Good night, Stan." Laughter follows her inside.

NINE

SAGE

SUNDAY MORNING FINDS me at the ranch for one of my weekly volunteer shifts. I feed the pygmy goats their delicious chaffhaye. They gather around me like I'm handing out truffle fries. Maybe alfalfa hay is the equivalent? I smell the bucket. Nope. Nothing delicious about that grassy scent.

Stan's proposal from last night runs through my head.

No, proposal is the very worst word for it.

Pretending to date sounds like a terrible idea.

Worse than Emma Stone's plan to be popular by faking being slutty in *Easy A*.

It can only end badly.

For me.

The petty, revengeful part of me who pretends she's Uma in the *Kill Bill* movies thinks it might be fun to watch Landon squirm. She assumes he'd notice or care.

I ask myself why I care what he thinks.

I don't.

Anymore.

Being Stan's fake girlfriend, I'd be the envy of the horny

hordes who follow him around like these goats gathered at my feet.

I'm not sure how he thinks it will help me find a good man, but he was pretty convincing dating him will weed out the arseholes and insecure losers.

His damn accent makes everything sound better.

Even ridiculous ideas like this one.

I sprinkle the last of the feed from my bucket and the goats stare at me, waiting for more.

"All done. No more," I tell them like they can understand English. I even show them the empty bucket and turn it upside down to prove my point. "Finito."

A black and white one named Oreo head-butts my calf.

"Listen, buddy. There's some right over there." I point behind him.

He blinks his weird vertical goat eyes at me and lets out a long, disgusted "blaaah" at my suggestion.

I walk over to a small pile of hay the others missed. He follows and bounces ahead of me when he sees it.

"You're welcome," I say.

He ignores me, happily chewing away with his mouth open. The rude bugger.

Inside the barn, I replace the bucket in the proper bin. Pacey the donkey sticks his head out of the stall and brays at me. "You're next, mister."

What's with all the demanding beasts this morning? Usually Sundays are mellow at the ranch. I feel like I'm serving brunch at the Ritz on Mother's Day for all the attitude these animals are showing me.

I pull a carrot from my overalls. Pacey's old and will probably spend the rest of his days here at the ranch. It's a pretty good life for a grumpy old man like him. Typically on Sundays, I bring a couple carrots or apples for Pacey and any horses we have.

He happily chomps it from my hand while I scratch by his ears. The old man leans into my touch and allows me to rub his soft nose. More dog in personality than horse, he reminds me of a Norwich terrier my mother had when we were little. Petunia Blum lived the life of royalty. My sister and I were her ladies in waiting.

Feeding duties finished, I check the stalls. Mucking out isn't my favorite thing. Okay, it's my very least favorite. I'm relieved to see fresh straw in Pacey's area. Someone's already done the gross work for me.

I cut across the goat pen on my way to the main building. Oreo and his buddies optimistically bounce around me and topple over each other. I show them my completely empty hands. "Nothing up my sleeves, fellas."

I feel rather than see Oreo's head butt on my other calf. I might have a bruise from his horns. If I knew how to knit, I'd make him colorful cozies for them.

Carefully closing the gate behind me, I double-check the latch. We had a break out earlier this year. Found two goats on the roof of the shed. Eight feet off the ground and no idea how they got up there.

Crazy goats.

Even crazier is me for considering Stan's offer.

How authentic would this deception be? Would there be kissing? Handholding? Would we go full out friends with benefits? Is he expecting sex? We're already seen around town together. He's drooled on my throw pillows.

I need more details.

Rules.

The guys all know about the "list" at the club.

Is this a big prank?

His comment about Hannibal and the elephants did make me laugh last night. Not enough to blindly say yes.

Inside the office, I find Elizabeth, the ranch manager, and two volunteers from Basalt. They're talking about a litter of puppies coming into the shelter after being found with their mamma in an abandoned barn down valley.

"Puppies always bring joy to the ranch," Elizabeth murmurs, a familiar look in her eyes.

"You can't adopt another dog. You have five at home," I say as I wash my hands in the little kitchen.

"We'll need to find foster homes for them once they're weaned. For now we'll set up the mom and pups in the back room where they'll be cozy and safe. Poor mamma is probably a runaway or a stray."

Elizabeth's heart is bigger than any other human I've ever met. She used all the money from her husband's life insurance to buy this land with the sole purpose of rescuing animals and giving the non-adoptable ones a good life. She lives in a small house on the far side of her multi-acre property surrounded by rolling hills.

With every animal that comes to the ranch, her menagerie grows. Her five dogs are all rescues, ranging from a Great Pyrenees mix to a mutt named Mr. Clean who resembles a rope mop. Besides Pacey and the goats, she has a pot-bellied pig named Grace and too many chickens to name or count.

I flip on the kettle for tea. "I might be able to take a couple of puppies. My teaching schedule usually has breaks during the day so they wouldn't be left alone for more than a few hours."

"Will the owner of your condo mind you having dogs? Some of the nicer complexes in town are very strict about pets," Mary, the older of the two other volunteers points out. Her tone tells me she thinks I'm a spoiled girl for living in Aspen. I don't need or want to tell her my parents own my condo and feed into her disdain.

"Oh, they're totally cool about dogs. They love dogs."

"You might want to double-check your lease. I'm happy to take the mom and all the puppies. I'm retired and own my house. We have a fenced yard, too."

Is she puppy-blocking me? The puppies haven't even arrived yet and she's going all Cruella De Vil over wanting *all* the puppies.

Any woman wearing a sweatshirt with a tutu sporting Chihuahua on the front is not to be trusted.

Elizabeth must sense the tension in the room. She gives me a sympathetic smile. "Let's see what the situation is when they arrive. We probably have more than enough puppies to go around, Mary."

The kettle whistles, covering the "I'll take them all. All the puppies" comment I mutter under my breath.

Before five minutes ago, I didn't even want a dog, let alone puppies. But see if I let Greedy De Vil take them all.

Something clicks in my head. Maybe Stan is onto something with his idea. Being seen as taken could draw the normal guys out of their hiding places.

Or more crazies.

My car is warm from the sun, reminding me summer is coming.

A shadow passes over my windshield and a hawk screeches before diving into a field outside the gate, disappearing into the tall grass.

I say a quick prayer for the little critter who is probably lunch.

Those inspirational quotes on Pinterest about the circle of life and one life pop into my head.

I text Stan before pulling out of the gravel parking area.

Hours later and he still hasn't responded.

Was he drunk last night and I didn't realize it? High on pain pills?

He seemed sober.

I can usually tell when he's had a few drinks. His accent gets stronger and he starts calling me *gogga*. I looked it up once. It means little bug. Not sure it's a compliment or a term for an annoying pest.

He's probably home. I'm his driver. Where else could he be? I resist knocking on his door after I park the Jeep.

I'm humming along to Taylor Swift on the radio and have to wait for the song to finish before going inside. The woman knows about complicated relationships with men.

"Sing it, sister." I raise my hands to give her props. She can't see me, but it doesn't matter. She feels the love.

After the song and our duet finishes, I jump out and leave the car in my driveway. I catch movement in Stan's front window and pause.

I'm holding my breath, standing in front of our doors.

We haven't even begun this thing and already I'm acting differently.

I'm doomed.

His door opens and his shaggy head pops out. "Hello, *gogga*."

I wave and drop my keys. He steps out on his crutches to help me, but he's too slow.

"I got your text. Want to come over and talk?"

I'm still bent over and I peek at him around my legs. He's completely staring at my ass. I'm still wearing overalls from working at the ranch earlier. Not sure how much he can see, but his focus heats my skin.

"Sure." I straighten up and try to nonchalantly toss my keys to catch them. I miss and they land at his feet.

So smooth.

With a chuckle, he swoops down, balancing on his good leg to scoop them up.

As I pass him in the doorway, I can smell his clean soapy smell. His hair is in its bun, but a few damp strands have escaped.

"Have you been hanging out with livestock, Farmer Girl?" He pulls a small piece of straw from my braid.

"I was at the ranch."

"I can tell." He gestures to his face. "You have some dirt smudges."

I instantly regret my lurking. I should've parked in the garage and showered before talking to him.

"Maybe you should avoid sitting on any furniture though. Wouldn't want you to stink up the place." He thumps past me to the sofa and sprawls out on the chaise section.

"Oh, please. A little hay and goat essence might freshen up the place." I settle into his armchair.

"Goats, you say? My great-grandparents and grandparents were Boers and had a large farm in Kwazulu Natal. Mostly cattle, but goats and sheep are everywhere in South Africa. Are these dairy goats?"

"Pygmy. There are five of them currently on the ranch."

"I should come with you sometime."

"We're getting puppies." My voice rises with excitement.

He raises a dark eyebrow. "We?"

"Elizabeth at the ranch. Someone found a mamma with her litter in an old barn."

"Okay, you worried me a little. I'm not sure our fake relationship is ready for the pet stage."

"I might be fostering some. If Cruella doesn't take them all with her fenced yard and retirement checks."

"You volunteer with a woman named Cruella?"

"From *101 Dalmatians*?"

He stares at me blankly.

"The Disney cartoon? Evil woman with black and white hair? Steals puppies to make a coat?"

His expression morphs through confusion to shock to disgust. "This is a children's movie?"

"You've never seen it?"

"Not a Yank, *gogga*. Remember?"

"What were you busy doing in your childhood? Other than suppressing the natives with your colonial tyranny?"

He glowers at me. "Low."

"Too soon?"

"Do you really want me to go over the history of South Africa again? Last time your eyes glazed over and you nearly fell asleep before I even got to the Second Boer War."

I fake a yawn. "If I don't remember the First Boer War, how can I jump in to the second one?"

He scowls. "Typical American."

"I'm teasing. Although you're right about Americans knowing world history. Most of us only paid attention to Nelson Mandela and refer to the continent as one giant country called Africa."

With a sigh, he changes the subject. "To answer your question, I was probably playing with goats on my grandparents' farm instead of being brainwashed by American culture."

"Didn't protect you. Not at all. You're practically one of us now." I begin to softly chant, "One of us, one of us. USA. USA."

"*Malkoppie poppie*," he curses under his breath.

"Did you call me crazy in Afrikaans?"

He smiles. "Ah, so you are learning something of my culture. *Malkoppie* does mean crazy. I'm proud of you, *skattebol*."

"And you lost me again. Skate ball doesn't sound flattering."

"How about *mooi skat*? Better?"

"Scat me? So much worse. That cannot be a compliment."

"It means beautiful darling."

"No way. It's something dirty and you want me to repeat it in public. Like the time you told me to tell Easley to vulcan duff po pole."

He snorts. *"Vokken dof poepol."*

With his smooth accent, the Dutch based Afrikaans rolls of his tongue like seduction.

"What does it mean?"

"Fucking dumb asshole."

I try to repeat the phrase to memorize it. "Vulcan doff po pole."

"Close enough. Your Afrikaans accent is terrible."

"Thank you. So is your American." It's not. Not even close. If he's not being charming, or tipsy, I barely hear it anymore. It's a crime against women he doesn't use it all the time. Although, how would we get anything done around him? Would we even care?

TEN

STAN

ONCE AGAIN, WE'RE completely off track on a random tangent. I'd been listening for Sage's Jeep to pull up so I could invite her over. I didn't want to discuss this via text.

Now she has me teaching her Afrikaans cursing, which she's butchering.

"You were telling me about the puppies? What kind are they?" I had a dog when I was little, but he stayed behind with my mum when I came to the States. Training and moving around with my father weren't conducive to getting a pet of any kind. Or so he always told me.

"I don't know. They're arriving from the vet tomorrow. I'm thinking about fostering one or two." Her eyes light up with the thought. "Want to help me?"

"Crutches and puppies don't mix."

"How much longer are you on those things?"

"Not sure. I have a doctor's appointment tomorrow at ten forty-five. Want to take me?"

"I have barre at nine. I can swing by and get you after. Will that work?"

"Perfect. I'll take you out for a late breakfast as a thank you."

"Main Street?"

"Where else? We can start the charade then."

She stills.

"Are you having second thoughts?"

Playing with the end of her braid and not looking at me, she shakes her head. "No. I guess I didn't realize it would be a full time thing."

"I'm not talking living together or twenty-four-seven. But being seen together is part of the ruse, isn't it?"

She nods and meets my eyes.

Attempting to reassure her, I ask, "What's going to be any different than all the other times we've hung out?"

"Will there be touching?" Her voice is soft and she sounds nervous.

"I imagine there will be. We touch already. Would be weird to stop now."

She nods again, pulling the corner of her bottom lip under her teeth. When she releases it, the color deepens. It's mesmerizing.

I read in a men's magazine once that a woman's lip color corresponds to her nipple color. I don't only read men's and rugby magazines, but sometimes I learn something when I do.

Important things like now being able to imagine Sage's nipple color.

She's speaking, but I've lost the thread of the conversation again.

"Hmm?" I ask, subtly shifting myself after imagining her breasts and nipples.

My thoughts about her have shifted. I jerked off after she offered to wash my back. Taking things in hand in the shower, so to speak, is nothing new, but typically I don't focus on Sage.

Or I didn't.

Now I'm sitting here thinking about her nipples and feel my body responding as I imagine her topless.

My brilliant idea to have a laugh and buy myself some peace from unwanted attention in the quiet off-season might not be so brilliant. Not if I'm being honest with myself. I want to spend more time with her. What I don't want is her dating some loser.

And not me.

"Are you listening?" Her words bring me back.

"Sorry." I give her a small smile.

"PDA?"

"The golf association? The PGA?" Another one of her tangents?

"No, public display of affection. I assume that's what you have planned for us."

"Sure. Are you talking about handholding or tongue kissing?"

Her eyes widen for a split second with surprise. Or excitement. Before I can analyze it, the look is gone.

"When was the last time you made out in public? Seems out of character."

"Then you don't remember the pap pics of me and the hotel heiress at the Jerome's New Year's Eve party a few years ago." Not one of my finest moments and thanks to the internet, it lives on forever.

"Are you serious? How did I not know about this?"

"I think it was before you moved here."

She pulls her phone out of the front pocket of her overalls. "What should I enter?"

"You're kidding, right? Stalk me online on your own time. We have business to discuss." I sit up straighter and put my good foot on the floor. "What are you nervous about?"

"Who said I was nervous? I'm not nervous. Calm, cool

cucumber."

"Okay, then. Want to practice our kissing now?" I shouldn't tease her, but it's impossible to resist. I run my tongue along the inside of my bottom lip to wet it. "You'll have to come to me given my gimp status."

She flails her hands in front of her face and over her head. "Be serious!"

"I am." I pull a frown. "See?"

"Handholding is fine. Palm on the lower back is okay. General touching. A kiss on the cheek."

"Only one cheek? The left or the right?" My smile turns wolfish. "Or did you mean my arse?"

Her cheeks deepen with color.

"Are you planning to be this—"

"Charming?"

"Incorrigible."

I pretend to glower at her. "You say that like it's a negative."

With a sigh she closes her eyes and shakes her head. "What madness have I agreed to?"

"It's going to be fun. I promise. We'll laugh for years about this."

"Or the entire thing will snowball into an avalanche."

Sitting in the waiting room at the orthopedist, I take Sage's hand in mine. I'm thrilled when she doesn't immediately snatch it way. I study the back and her short nails, then turn it over to trace my finger over the lines of her palm.

"What does my lifeline say?" she whispers.

"You're the crunchy one. Maybe you should tell me." I flip my palm up so she's cradling my hand.

"I'm not a psychic."

"Give it a go."

With her middle finger, she traces the thick line down the middle. "You'll have a long life."

"What about my love life?" I close my fist around her finger for a moment and open it again.

She points at two parallel lines. "It's one of these. I'm sure it says you'll have many lovers."

"Will I get married? Children?"

Tapping the middle line, she says, "At least a dozen."

"Children or marriages?"

Our gazes meet.

"Do you want multiple marriages?"

I shake my head. "No. One should do fine."

With a lift of her eyebrow, she silently questions me.

"It's true. You never believe me, but under this ultra-cool bun is a one woman, one marriage for life kind of man."

I'm certain she doesn't believe me. After living next door to me for two years, she's seen the parade of women. Sure, I date. I have casual sex. I never lead a woman to think there will be more when there won't be. Everyone plays by the rules and no one gets hurt.

Except in life—like in rugby—there are people who will play dirty, who will cheat, and twist things to their own advantage. I'm not a prize to be won and set upon a shelf. Or bragged over at the bar. Or worse, on social media.

I liked the hotel heiress. Until I realized the pap photos were intentional and I was a pawn to get back at her boyfriend, some Eurotrash DJ.

"I believe you," Sage softly whispers.

The X-ray technician calls me and I leave Sage behind.

A short while later, I'm sporting a black walking cast and a shiny silver cane. I twirl it to make Sage laugh and waddle around the waiting area like a silent movie.

"Look at you, sporty. How much longer until you're back in shoes?" she asks as we pull out of the parking lot. My crutches are tossed in the back seat.

"A month in the boot, only a few weeks in this lovely thing. I can start real physical therapy next week." I've been doing flexibility work with bands and resistance with my trainer at home. Nothing weight bearing, but he gave me a few exercises to stave off any muscle atrophy. "The orthopedist reminded me how lucky I am that it was only a hairline fracture and nothing worse. He told me some horror stories about Pilon fractures and dislocations."

"I'm sure he's seen it all. Could've been worse." Sage's stomach growls.

"Main Street Bakery, hungry girl?"

"I'm starving. I only ate a cup of yogurt before class."

One of the things I love about Sage is her appetite. She's never been one of those girls to exist on air and the garnishes in her cocktails.

With the cane, I can walk beside her and open the door for her. Like a gentleman. Like a man dating her.

Entering the cafe, I place my palm on her lower back and she startles before giving me a shy smile over her shoulder. I return her smile and keep contact, feeling her warmth through her purple fleece jacket. The color and texture remind me of a Teletubby.

We say hello to a few familiar faces before settling ourselves at a table in the back of the white-painted farmhouse style café.

"Nice move with the hand." She peers over her menu at me.

"You like that? There's more where that came from." I run my hand down her arm. "Especially when you dress like a stuffed animal."

Her laughter is easy and light. "I can get you a matching jacket. We could be one of those couples who insist on dressing alike."

"Even better if we're the type who dresses alike and doesn't realize it. We're that in synch." I wink at her.

Livia stands beside our table and greets us. "Hey guys. How's the leg, Lee?"

I proudly show her my new boot and cane before we order. I get a Denver scramble and Sage orders the loaded home fries with a side of fruit.

"You two are the cutest," Livia says. "It's about time you started dating."

She leaves us to grab our coffees.

Sage and I widened our eyes as we stare at each other.

"About time?" she asks. "What does that mean?"

"Our plan is working better than I thought."

ELEVEN

STAN

"HEARD YOU AND Sage were having a morning after meal together at Main Street yesterday." Easley relentlessly flips through channels with my remote.

The guys have invaded my space to watch the last qualifying round of sevens for the Olympics on my television.

If we're not at Little Annie's, we typically gather at my place because I don't have a dozen roommates and it's the tidiest. As in I have someone who comes to clean and I own a vacuum.

My screen is also the largest.

I'm not a sizest. It's the truth.

Landon sets his glass down heavily on the coffee table.

I wait for him to comment on Easley's gossip.

"I thought she was on the club list?" Landon's voice is deliberately flat. He doesn't fool me.

"I added it and I can take it off. So I did."

"You totally did that on purpose! Brilliant. Why didn't I think of that? You cockblock the rest of us and then swoop in and fuck her yourself." *Vokken* Easley and his rude mouth.

"First of all, we're not fucking." It's the truth.

"Ooh, making love. Excuse me." Easley prances around to the other chair not occupied by Landon.

He's preoccupied with cramming pretzels into his mouth while staring out the window. "Speaking of fucking, Tess is a freak in the bedroom."

Easley gives him a thumbs up. "I can totally see that. What's Sage like?"

I flash my eyes over to Landon, who barely meets my glance. I dare him to make a comment about her.

"Come on, dude. That's like crossing-swords. You can't talk about a woman who's been with two guys in the same room." Landon shudders.

This is a new chapter in the bro-code. One I'm grateful for. I'd probably have to tackle Landon and throw him out if he started giving his opinion on Sage in bed.

Mostly because the thought burns through me with a mix of anger and jealousy. I sound like a broken record, but I still can't believe she ever dated him. Let alone got naked with him.

I can't think of anyone less deserving of a woman like her.

"Where's your girlfriend? Shouldn't she be glued to your side?" Easley jokes.

"The nice thing about living next door to her is all I have to do is knock on the wall."

"Man, that's the life. Sex on demand, but not having to deal with all her girl crap all over your house." Easley continues digging his hole.

"But what happens when it ends? Then your ex is right there." Landon points at the joint wall. "Hope you have good insulation and sound-proofing."

"Who says it's going to end?" I cross my arms.

The two of them break into big guffaws.

"Right," they say simultaneously.

"When have you ever had a girlfriend?" Landon gives me a sidelong look.

My relationship isn't even real and I'm defensive about it. "Fuck off. Sage is different."

"Is she really?" Landon snarks. "Thought she was pretty basic under all the hippie shit."

I stand and pick up the empty pretzel bowl to avoid punching him. "Okay. New subject."

They finally clue in I'm serious, and shut up when the match starts.

I have no idea what happens on the pitch other than the final score at the end. Possessive thoughts and jealousy occupy my mind. Fake relationship or not, I'm not going to let the likes of Landon and Easley near Sage ever again.

I knock and let myself into Sage's condo. "Hello?"

"In the kitchen!"

The vision of her stops me a few feet from the door.

Beyoncé blasts out of the speakers and flour covers the kitchen island. Or powdered sugar. The scent of coconut and apricot fill the air.

"What are you making?" The whole condo smells of *Hertzoggies*, my absolute favorite sweet in the world. I don't dare to hope.

"It's a surprise." She blocks the oven.

I glance at the timer. Ten minutes to wait. I take a seat on one of her barstools. Where not sprinkled in flour, mail and random papers cover her counter.

"Who is Gertrude Blum and why do you have her mail?" I hold up an envelope with a Chicago law firm as the return address. "Are you stealing someone's mail?"

She grabs it and stuffs it in a random drawer in the kitchen. "It's a Federal crime to tamper with the mail."

"So that's a no on the thievery? Is it for your grandmother?"

"She's dead. I've told you that before."

"It all could be lies at this point. My final guess, and you can nod yes if you are afraid we're being recorded, is you are living life on the lam." I nod yes to demonstrate to her how to do it. Not that I don't think she understood me, but I know my exaggerated antics will make her laugh.

She nods, then switches to shaking her head no. "You watch too many mafia movies and crime shows."

"Only *Goodfellas*. As a young boy growing up in Cape Town, Ray Liotta taught me the value of hard work in America."

"That's twisted on so many levels I don't know where to begin."

My eyes flash to the drawer she's protecting. "It's always the innocent ones who turn out to be the most dangerous."

She steps away from the drawer and tidies up the mess on the counter. "The Midwest is the cradle of all that is wholesome in America. Like John Hughes movies."

"Did you grow up in Chicago? Or in one of those corn fields visible as the plane flies over the country?"

"Chicago. North side."

"I loved Ferris Bueller as a kid." I don't tell her my father lives on an obnoxiously high floor in the same building as Oprah in Chicago. I'd rather not discuss Stanley Barnard, senior.

"Just when I thought you were hopeless with American pop culture you drop Goodfellas and Ferris Bueller in a matter of minutes. There might be hope for you yet."

I match her easy smile with my own. "Good to know you haven't ruled me out, *gogga*."

"Calling me a little bug doesn't help your cause."

I slap my hands on the edge of the counter like I'm playing the bongos. It's a term of endearment, but I'm not sure I should tell her that. "*Gogga* has the same first letter as Gertrude. Could be a coincidence."

Sighing, she peeks inside the oven. I lean forward to catch a glimpse, but she blocks me with her back. Instead, I stare at the curve of her ass in her yoga shorts. They're more like underwear with the way they cling to her body, revealing her strong dancer's legs. At home we call them *sjoebroekies*.

"My real name is Gertrude," she whispers.

"I'm sorry, can you repeat that?" I cup my hand around my ear. "I swear you said your name is Gertrude."

"Listen, Stanley, you shouldn't toss rocks inside your glass house."

"What's the story behind Sage?"

"Try going through life as a teenager named Gertrude. In the twenty-first century."

I chuckle. "Gertrude and Stanley. We make a striking pair. In Sun City."

"I was going to say Scottsdale. That's where my parents live."

"Where does Sage come from?"

"It's my middle name. Rose is really Edith. The parental Blums went through a Phish-following hippie phase after college. So Sage and Rose we are."

"Edith's not bad. What's with the old-fashioned names?"

"We were named for great grandmothers. It's a tradition to name a baby after a deceased relative."

"Is this an American tradition?"

"Jewish."

"Really? I didn't know."

"Why would you? I don't know your religion despite staring at a zoomed in picture of your shorts."

I choke on nothing.

"I'm kidding. You can't tell someone's religion from staring at their junk. Or their physical attributes. Although, the family joke is my mom had a wild affair with the blond mailman. Everyone else in the family has brown or red hair. My coloring comes from my Norwegian grandmother."

"Your family jokes about your mom cheating on your father?"

"If you knew my parents, you'd see how ridiculous the idea is. They're one of those couples who act like they're newly in love. It can be disgusting."

"Wow."

"I know." She gets a faraway look in her eyes. "It's a lot of pressure to find 'the one' and have their kind of lifelong love."

"What about Rose?"

"She and Archie have a great relationship. He worships her and she thinks he walks on water. Sorry, Jesus joke."

"No offense."

"They met first week of college. The rest fell into place exactly as Rose planned when she set her life goals at thirteen, including having her first baby at twenty-six. She's right on schedule."

"Impressive. And you?"

"I'm the white sheep in a herd of black ones. The dreamer, my father calls me. It's not really a compliment."

"It should be. The world needs more dreamers." This is the most we've ever talked about her family. I want to know more, but I don't ask. Because what if she wants to hear about my parents? I'm fine talking about my mum. She's my favorite person on the planet.

"My mum will love hearing that an American girl baked for me. She thinks everyone here is on a diet or only eats fast food."

With a shy smile, she pulls a tray out of the oven. "I'm not sure they're any good."

Small tarts line the tray. The coconut and apricot smell is joined by melted sugary butter. It's too good to be true.

"Am I dreaming?"

She carefully moves them to a wire cooling rack with a spatula. I reach out to grab one, burning my fingers on the hot crust.

I give the hot tart a dirty look. Having something I want so desperately this close and not being allowed to touch it is the worst kind of torture.

Unable to stay away, I lean down and inhale the aroma. "Hello, my *Liefie*. I've missed you."

"Are you talking to food now?" Sage leans over the counter so her head is close to mine. She giggles. "Whispering sweet nothings?"

Our foreheads are inches apart. When she exhales her minty breath combines with mine. Beneath the coconut-apricot scent, I can smell her floral shampoo. It's a heady combination. If I shift my head . . .

She tilts hers at the same time.

"Ouch!" She rubs her forehead where it collided with mine. "Do you have a metal plate in your head?"

I press my fingers against my head. "No. Do you?"

"Is it swelling?" She lifts her hair to reveal her forehead. There's nothing there. Not even a red mark.

"No, but do you want me to kiss it to make it better?" I don't expect her to take me seriously after our touching versus no-touching talk last week.

Nor do I think she'll lean forward and pause. Is she—?

"Well. Are you going to make it better?"

I gently brush my lips along her hairline and inhale her scent.

It would be so easy to lift her chin and properly kiss her. So easy.

I pause, gathering myself to blast through the wall dividing our friendship from something more.

In that moment, she shifts away. "Much better."

I recover and grab a tart. The first bite nearly burns my mouth, but it's worth it. "Misisamashing."

"Is that Afrikaans for good?" She grins with pride.

I open my mouth to let out some of the heat, covering my chewing with my hand. After swallowing, I repeat the compliment. "This is amazing."

"Did I make it right?"

"Perfect."

"Good. I found the recipe online. I know they're probably not as good as your mum's or grandmother's, but I wanted to do something nice—"

I cut her off with my mouth.

TWELVE

STAN

I TANGLE MY fingers in her hair as I crash my lips on hers. She gasps and I sweep my tongue along her bottom lip, tasting her sweet mouth.

I move one arm behind her to pull her closer to me, but the corner of the counter separates us. Forced to adjust, I brace one hand on the cool granite. Sliding my body around the edge, I recapture her cheek with my hand. She's still kissing me. I don't want her to ever stop.

The need for oxygen tears my lips from hers. I inhale and trail my mouth down her neck.

"Stan," she whispers. "What are you doing?"

I smile against her soft skin. "Kissing you good and proper."

I weave our fingers together before pressing my lips against the back of her hand. A small shiver passes through her. I lift my eyes to meet hers, which are open wide.

I kiss the side of her mouth and give her a peck on the lips.

She's frozen and no longer responding to my touch.

"What's wrong?" I lean away to see her expression more clearly.

Her cheeks are flushed and her lips are plumper than normal. She blinks a few times, followed by a nervous laugh. "What's wrong?"

Our hands are still joined. I rub my thumb along the back of hers. "Nothing is wrong."

"We were kissing in my kitchen."

"Is it the kissing or the location you have issue with?" I tuck a stray hair behind her ear.

"You're so calm about this."

"I enjoyed it. Didn't you? Did I misread your body's reaction?" I drag my finger down her rosy cheek.

"That's not the point."

"If I'm rubbish at kissing, don't tell me. My delicate man ego can't handle the truth." It's intended to make her laugh and break this tension. When she doesn't respond and only stares at me blankly, a rabbit caught in headlights, I begin to panic.

"Sage?" I squeeze her hand.

"You're not rubbish."

I wipe my brow in relief. With a grin, I try to kiss her again. She leans away. "We should talk."

"No, I get it. I'm sorry. I overstepped." Her words are a cold shower. Dejected, I stuff my hands into my jeans and pick up my cane. I need a quick escape to maintain the lie of my calm façade. "I'll catch up with you later."

Her hand on my arm stops me from hobbling away like a sad troll. "Lee."

I face her and raise an eyebrow.

"You can't kiss me in the middle of the kitchen out of the blue. I . . . I wasn't prepared."

"I didn't plan it." I rub my pinkie finger along my bottom lip. "But I don't regret it."

"But . . . but . . . we're friends!" She points between us in case I don't know who she's talking about.

"And now we're friends who've kissed. Frankly, I'm amazed it hasn't happened sooner."

Her mouth opens and closes like she's trying to form words, then changing her mind before speaking. "Why would you? Think that?"

"Come on, it's never crossed your mind?" There's zero chance she hasn't thought about kissing me at least once. "Not even at the beginning? When we were strangers? Young, beautiful, and right there?"

"Those are great traits for falling in love." Her voice turns brittle.

"Who said anything about falling in love? I'm talking about two beautiful people hooking up in Aspen. Happens multiple times a day, every day of the year."

Her face tells me I've probably said the worst thing possible. I sound like my father.

"I didn't mean it like how it sounded. I'm not—" Not what? Trying to get laid? Not falling in love with her? Who even brought up love?

Oh, right. I did.

"I'm not using you. You made my favorite sweet and you look lovely. I didn't think. I had an overwhelming urge to kiss you. So I did."

I'd do it again in a heartbeat.

So I do.

Nothing aggressive. No tongue. I press my lips softly against her mouth and pull back after a few seconds. I stay close, our breaths intermingling.

She doesn't shove me away. "Stan . . ."

I hear the smile in her voice before I open my eyes and see her lips curve. She keeps her arms by her sides, but amusement sparks in her eyes.

I go in for another kiss, a quick sweep of my lips along hers. It's quickly becoming my favorite thing to do with her.

"Want me to stop?" I pause, again a breath away from her skin.

I inhale and she inhales. We exhale together.

"I—" Her ringing phone cuts off the rest of her sentence. "I should answer that. Zoe and I have plans later."

I lean back and give her space. While she answers her phone, I stuff the now cool tart into my mouth in two big bites. I moan around the taste of my childhood and home.

"Shh," she whispers. "It's the television. Some Channing Tatum movie. No, I'm not watching *Magic Mike XXL* without you."

I raise my eyebrows in question.

She waves me off.

I steal two more tarts and limp myself to the couch. Locating her remote in a basket on the wood coffee table, I flip on the TV, and lower the volume.

Her voice carries from the kitchen. I try not to eavesdrop. Instead, I snoop through her DVR. Sure enough *Magic Mike XXL* is recorded and waiting for her. I glance over my shoulder to see her back is turned.

Wondering if I can follow the plot of the sequel having not seen the original one, I hit play.

"Well, well, well. So this is what women watch instead of porn," I mumble to myself.

If they expect regular guys to have these moves, and I'm talking dance moves that involve the ability to roll their hips while thrusting, they're going to be sadly disappointed by most real men.

Even with a fully functioning ankle, I'm not sure I could

do half those things, and I'm a super fit athlete.

I finish off the second tart and look longingly at the rest on the tray so far away.

My phone buzzes in my shirt pocket. I extract it and swipe my finger. My trainer Chris wants to schedule some more physical therapy sessions. I respond and we set a date for tomorrow morning. I hope Sage can drive me.

She's still whispering on the phone. With a glance over her shoulder, she catches me staring and ends the conversation.

"Can you bring me another tart? Or two? Maybe three?" I point at the tray and then myself. "They're too far away."

"How many have you had already?"

"Only three."

"Only?" She obliges me and places three on a paper towel before joining me on the couch.

"Thank you."

She picks up a tart and takes a bite. A few small crumbs remain on her lip as she chews. I resist licking them off for her.

"Are you watching Magic Mike?" Her gaze flicks from me to the TV and back.

"When you mentioned it on the phone, I realized I've never seen this gem of American cinema. You're always teasing me about my lack of pop culture knowledge."

"In that case, we're going to need more tarts." In the kitchen she opens a cupboard and pulls out a glass. "Want some milk?"

I make a sour face. "No thanks. Only Americans and toddlers drink milk straight up in a glass."

"Suit yourself. Water?"

"Please."

Whatever awkward tension my spontaneous kiss created seems to dissipate. At least on the surface. When she returns and sits close enough for me to feel her body heat, but too far away to be touching me, I lose track of the movie.

I'm sure there's a very deep plot about the plight of male dancers and the women who love them in XXL. A stripper with a heart of gold is an iconic bit of American storytelling.

Instead I focus on Sage's profile and her lips as she eats another tart. Her tongue darts out to catch a stray crumb and I nearly pounce on her. A bit of apricot jam spills on her fingers and she sucks it off, sweeping her tongue along the side of the pad of her thumb.

I am transfixed by her.

I've always thought she was beautiful, ethereal. She's amazingly fit and graceful. But until recently, I haven't lusted after her. Now sitting next to her is torture. I can't even come up with anything to tease her about.

I finally think of something to say to snap my mind out of the bedroom. "Can you drive me to PT tomorrow morning?"

"I have back to back classes from eight to ten."

I frown. I should've checked with her before agreeing to Chris's new schedule. "That won't work."

"What time is your appointment?"

"Ten."

"I can pick you up after. Call one of the guys or Darren to get you."

Of course it's not a big deal, but I'm cranky now.

"No problem. I'll figure out a ride both ways." Pouting, I stretch out my legs and rest them on the coffee table. "Is Zoe going to be mad you watched this without her?"

Her laugh turns into a snort. "We've already seen it multiple times. Once in the theater and then streaming. It's almost a weekly thing for us."

I smirk at her. "Why does this surprise me?"

"Have you met us? Zoe loves herself some man candy."

"And you?"

"I'm female and breathing."

Her comment does nothing to dispel my crankiness.

"Oh, stop. You're my favorite man candy." She leans her head on my shoulder. Her hair smells like coconut from her baking.

"Thank you for making me the Hertzoggies."

"Anytime."

THIRTEEN

SAGE

STAN, HIS MAN bun, and I are snuggling on my sofa. Before the snuggling, we were making out in the kitchen. I pinch myself to confirm I'm awake. After crushing on him for two years, I can now happily say he's an amazing kisser. There's a good chance we're going to have sex. At some point. Not tonight. I haven't shaved my legs in days and let's just say my legs aren't the only area needing grooming. Honestly, I've let things slide during my self-inflicted celibacy. If a bush grows and no one is there to see it, does it really exist? I make a note to schedule a waxing appointment this week.

I can smell his soap and maybe shampoo; both are manly without being overpowering. He smells clean and a little spicy.

My head rests on his shoulder while he plays with my hair. It's soothing and exhilarating because Stan is touching me. He hasn't stopped touching me since he kissed me silent in the kitchen.

Making out in the kitchen with Stan the Man Bun.

If I keep focusing on how amazing I felt kissing him, I won't freak out I was kissing him.

"Why do you insist on calling me Stan?" he asks.

"It helps me keep you contained."

"Why would you want to contain me?"

Not him per se. More like my feelings for him. "You need someone to keep things real and not overfeed your ego. Stan is far less sexy than Lee."

"Kind of like Sage is far sexier than Gertrude?"

"Shh. You promised to keep my secret, Stanley."

"Matching outfits," he whispers.

"We'll make a fine pair." A pair of what is the question.

There is only one letter separating Stan from Satan.

Coincidence?

Deep in my bones I know I have no one to blame but myself. However, when the devil sets his charms on a girl, it takes a burning bush to resist his evil ways.

I'm not talking a STD. More in the biblical sense. I think. I'm not one-hundred-percent on the burning bush Bible reference being accurate. We're more High Holiday and a good bagel nosh kind of Jews. My knowledge of the Old Testament is vague at best.

Since college, I'm more of a lapsed Buddhist of the Namaste and hot yoga variety.

In other words, nothing.

No wonder I have no defense against Satan with a South African accent.

Not when he shows up at the ranch later in the week. Then sits on the ground to play with the newly arrived puppies.

It's not fair. He's sitting there in the dirt, letting himself be a jungle gym for the cutest balls of fur I've ever seen. I'm trying to think of when he's looked more handsome.

He doesn't seem to care he's getting dirty.

I care.

His white T-shirt stretches over his back and biceps every time he moves. It leaves little to the imagination. Thank whatever god or saint is in charge of clothing. And rugby.

And dogs.

"How old are they?" He leans back as two brown fluff-balls try to scale his chest. A peek of skin shows between his jeans and T-shirt.

I shift my weight on my feet, causing one dog to attack my sneaker's laces. "The vet says about four weeks."

"They're big for being that young."

"The vet thinks they're some type of retriever and Husky mixes. Probably Lab. Maybe Malamute."

"Are we taking one?" He holds up his arm where a fat bellied puppy is clamped onto his T-shirt sleeve and pulling with all his strength.

I glance around to make sure we don't have an audience. "Cruella has generously offered to foster the mom and all six puppies."

Frowning, he shifts the puppy off his sleeve and into his lap where she tumbles over onto her back. "That seems a little greedy."

I agree. "It's probably best for the dogs to stay together for a little while longer."

"When are they up for adoption?"

"In another three to four weeks after they get their shots."

Stan picks up one of the boys, who is black and gray, with a white blaze across his forehead. "You have my sympathies, little man."

The runt, and my personal favorite, has given up clamoring for Satan's attention. Smart girl. Instead, she's toddled over to the fence near the goats. Three goats blink their weird eyes at her, not sure if she's friend of foe.

She barks. They scatter, but don't go far, keeping their attention focused on her.

"Are the goats adoptable?" Laughter brightens his voice.

"Where are you going to put a goat?"

"The back patio?" He shrugs with a shy smile.

"I'm sure there are city ordinances forbidding goats in condos and association by-laws stating the same."

"That weird guy at the end of our row of condos has a ferret."

"Not the same thing."

He rolls his bottom lip in an exaggerated pout. "Doesn't seem fair."

"Maybe you should buy a ranch."

"With all my millions in the bank from modeling?"

Or with mine, I think.

"Fine. No goats, but we could get a puppy. Share the responsibilities."

"You want to have joint custody on a dog? What happened to it being too soon in our fake relationship for dogs?" I pick up the puppy as she tries to wiggle under the fence to get to her new goat friends. She squirms until I sit her upright in my arms, then she rewards me with a face lick.

"Pfft. That was weeks ago. We're ready. Our schedules never line up. When you're home, I'm bartending. When you're working, I'm sleeping or training. The dog would never be left alone for more than a couple of hours. Tops."

He makes a good point. "But we're not a real couple."

"What better way to legitimize us in the eyes of the world than adopting a dog together? It's one of the cornerstones of American relationships."

"Really?" I can't tell if he's serious.

"Of course. Right between going steady and betrothal. Or promised to be engaged."

"For someone who avoids relationships, you sound like an expert."

"Finishing school."

I almost drop the puppy. "Excuse me?"

"My father sent me to etiquette classes in New York when we moved there."

"Like which fork to use and how to curtsy?"

"Young gentlemen bow." He lifts an eyebrow at my faux pas. "Didn't you learn these things growing up in Chicago?"

"We were more the Hebrew school and Bat/Bar Mitzvahs crowd. I think maybe one day was spent on table manners. Dance classes since three."

"When does dance camp start? I'll need to add it to the puppy's schedule." He picks up the fat bellied one again. "What should we name you?"

"Who says that's the one we're getting. Look at this face." I hold up the runt in a Lion King pose.

"It's not all about looks, Sage." With a shake of his head, he scoops up as many puppies as he can hold in one arm, and stands. "We need a dog who is compatible to our lifestyles. Someone who can be a good companion, not only a pretty face and arm candy."

The puppies wriggle in his arms, trying to free themselves. All except the chubbiest one. He's perfectly content to be snuggled close to Stan. His eyes are closing; he's completely relaxed.

"Maybe we should get two. They can keep each other company when we're not there. If we ever have to move, we can divide them, and each have a dog."

"Like in *Parent Trap* when Lindsay Lohan plays twins? You

know that won't work. Someday they'll run into each other again at doggie day camp, realize they're siblings, and plot to bring us back together by switching places."

"You know the most random pop culture references for someone who swears he never paid attention to American culture."

Stan sets down all but the sleepy puppy, who flips onto his back and lolls his head back on Stan's arm. "It could happen."

My puppy is squirming to be set down with the others. I lower her to the ground and she rolls on her side before bouncing up and attacking a piece of straw.

"What? That we stop being neighbors or friends and have to split up the dogs?"

He regards me with horror. His mouth is open so wide, his bearded chin brushes his T-shirt. "What! No, not that part. That's never going to happen. I meant getting both dogs."

I wish I could believe him. Aspen is a stopover for more permanent places and lives. Most of our friends have a two to three year plan before they're off to new adventures or move to a big city for their real lives to begin.

"You're stuck with me," he says.

I expect a cheeky grin when I look up at him. It's not there. Instead, I find a serious faced Lee. "I almost believe you."

"Have a little faith. Now let's talk to Elizabeth about adopting some puppies."

Inside the office, we find Elizabeth sorting a tall stack of letters, some with checks attached. She greets us without stopping.

"What are all those?" Stan asks.

"Donations."

"Wow. They're so many of them." He scans the large table holding the bins from the post office.

"We're in the middle of our annual fundraising drive.

They're mostly small amounts. I'm grateful for every single one, but unless we get a couple large donors, they won't cover our operating expenses for six months."

This is news to me. I didn't realize how underfunded the ranch is. "That's all? I thought you funded everything."

She gives me a sympathetic smile. "I wish. I spent most of my money buying the land and building the structures. Feed and vet bills add up every month. Plus, there's maintenance on the buildings, taxes, and paying an accountant to tell me to raise more money."

"I had no idea."

"Why would you, Sage? You volunteer here a few hours a month. I typically don't share the financials with our volunteers. I want you to come and spend time with the animals, help with the adoptions. Not worry about money. That's my job." A small frown replaces her smile.

Listening to our conversation, Stan leans his weight against the doorframe. "We could do a fundraiser. Maybe with the rugby fest in the fall."

"Or a hot guys with dogs event. Who doesn't love that combination?" The words spill out of my mouth faster than I can think. "Or not."

Elizabeth laughs, a throaty chuckle. "I wouldn't want to impose on your handsome boyfriend."

He shoots me a fake glare, then turns up the charm. "I think it's a great idea. Only, Sage is missing half the market. We could do an event with some of Aspens most beautiful men *and* women. Perhaps a fun walk?"

"I like your thinking. There's a board meeting next week. Why don't the two of you draft something and present your ideas then?" Elizabeth writes something on a sticky note. "We could use some fresh faces and new ideas."

Stan scratches below his bun. "I don't really do board meetings. I'll hand this one over to Sage. She's more than capable."

"Oh, no you don't. We're a team." I poke his side.

"Meetings are the death of the soul," he grumbles.

"I agree with you there." Elizabeth gives him one of her kind smiles. She can get anyone to do anything with one of those smiles. "Anything else I can help you with?"

"We're adopting two of the puppies." It's not a question. His voice leaves no room for discussion.

"We?" She switches her focus from Stan to me. "Oh. I see."

I'm about to correct her, when he rests his arm around my shoulders. "Sage and I have hit the dog adopting stage of our relationship."

This news surprises her. "I didn't realize that was an official stage. Congratulations. Are you sure you want two?"

"They'll keep each other company," I say.

"Have you picked out the two you want? I'll give you first dibs. But don't tell Mary. She's very possessive of those dogs. Don't worry, I'll set her straight."

"Mary? I thought you said her name was Cruella?" Stan looks down at me.

"Cruella? De Vil?" Elizabeth's laugh fills the room. "Oh, that's perfect."

I smile, embarrassed, and then join her laughter.

We say our good-byes and walk out to the Jeep. Stan keeps his arm around me on the way to the car.

It's becoming pointless to keep thinking of him as Stan. The puppies trampled the power of the unsexy name to pieces. I give up. Satan, Stan, Lee, hell even Stanley, the name doesn't change my feelings for him. I'm doomed.

"We're getting puppies. This calls for a celebration. Can I buy you lunch at Woody Creek?"

"Is this a date?"

"Of course. We're celebrating the puppy stage." He squeezes my shoulder before releasing me to open my door.

"Did they teach you door opening at finishing school?"

He responds with a bow.

I'm still laughing at him as I drive down the bumpy dirt road.

FOURTEEN

SAGE

THE WEATHER IS nice enough to sit out on the patio at the tavern. Sheltered from the road by wood lattice, umbrellas shade a small cluster of tables. I pull on my fleece. I might have overshot the day's temperatures by wearing shorts.

"Is here okay, or would you rather be inside?" Lee asks.

I zip up my fleece. "Outside. The inside smells of tequila and the broken dreams of Hunter S. Thompson fanboys."

"But the Christmas lights and swags of T-shirts lining the ceiling are festive."

Woody Creek Tavern is as much a cultural institution as pilgrimage site and a place to have one of the best margaritas in the Roaring Fork valley. The Mexican food is good, too.

The legendary gonzo journalist died before either of us lived in Aspen, but from the stories being told daily at the tavern, I'd think he passed last year, or last week.

"Margaritas?" A dark-haired waitress hands us our menus. She's familiar, but I can't remember her name. She's also gorgeous with olive skin and wild, corkscrew curls

"Hey Liz," Lee greets her, pushing up his sunglasses.

"Lee! I didn't recognize you."

With your clothes on.

"Must be the cane."

Or seeing you in the daylight.

"Do you know Sage?"

My fake girlfriend.

"You teach barre in Aspen? I think I've taken one of your classes."

I've had wild, passionate sex with Lee.

"I do. You look familiar." The conversation in my head is more fascinating than this friendly and fake banter we all have going on.

"Yes on the margaritas? Extra salt, Lee?"

I know how he likes his drinks.

Lee stares at me. "Sure?"

"Make mine spicy." I touch his forearm across the table, tracing the lower edge of his tattoo.

"Okay. Let me put in those drinks and I'll be back to take your orders." Liz sashays away. A little too much roll to her hips for my liking.

"Spicy, eh?" Lee captures my hand in his and weaves our fingers together.

I nod. "You didn't hear the subliminal conversation we were having in my head about you. Have you slept with her?"

A slow, sexy smile lifts one corner of his mouth.

"What are you smiling about?"

"No, Liz and I have never slept together."

"I find that hard to believe."

"Why? I don't sleep with every woman I meet. I've known you for two years and haven't tried to sex you up, have I? I'm not some sort of untamed beast who can't control his sex drive."

"I don't count."

"So the answer to the rest of my question is yes, you do think I've slept with every other woman?"

"It's a small town. Women talk."

He leans forward, my hand trapped against the table by his. "Women gossip and lie."

"Way to stereotype a whole gender." I attempt to free my hand, but he doesn't let go.

"Some women do."

"And some men are promiscuous."

"Some. Not all." Releasing my hand, he relaxes back into his chair.

"Two margaritas, one spicy, one extra salt." Liz sets down our glasses. Thin slices of jalapeño float on the surface of mine.

Here's a view of my cleavage in case you forgot it.

I throw shade at the low cut of her top and then side-eye Lee.

"How's Jane?" Lee asks, while staring at me.

"She's great. She has a gig playing piano at the Snowmass Club all summer. You two should stop by some night. I'm working the rodeo on Wednesday. Come to that and then we'll go have a drink after."

Drink is code for . . . wait. Jane?

"Jane's a big fan of your classes, Sage. She says her butt has never looked better and I have to agree."

My brows furrow and lift as I process her words. "Jane Sills is your . . ."

"Wife." She lifts her left hand to show off a blue stone set in a silver band. "We're newlyweds."

Lee chuckles.

"Liz and Jane have been together for years. They're one of the few truly happy couples I know." His eyes tell me he's biting his tongue to keep from laughing at my stupid jealousy.

We order food and Liz checks on other tables. Sipping my

margarita through my straw, I study the fascinating lattice pattern.

"Green is a lovely color on you, Sage."

"Har har. Sage. Sage green."

He taps my fingers with his. "I meant the jealousy."

"Of course you did. Your ego probably feeds on it, and the tears of women whose hearts you've broken."

"I don't break hearts. I never lead a woman on." He believes what he's saying. I can tell by the earnest tone to his voice.

"No, you probably don't. Their hearts go willingly along, basking in your glory, then throw themselves into the ravine when they realize they can't have you."

"Dramatic much?" He laughs again. Flipping my hand over, he traces the lines of my palm. "You're not the ravine type, are you?"

He holds my heart in his hands as well as my palm, but I'm not going to tell him that. I know exactly what I'm doing here.

Being a fool.

Playing with fire.

Falling in love with my best friend.

After lunch the day is too beautiful to go home. I take a right instead of heading into town and wind my way up to the Maroon Bells. The three red peaks are snow-capped, even in summer. A few other cars fill the parking lot, but I find a spot for the Jeep near the hiking trail.

We can't have a real hike with Lee still in his boot, but the path around the lake is flat enough I could push him in a wheelchair if I had to.

We pass by another couple and their pair of Golden Retrievers.

"In a few months, that will be us. Our dogs will be expert hikers. We'll train them to carry their own packs and water. Maybe they can even work for the ski company as avalanche dogs." He sounds eager and excited.

"I'm not sure they'll be avalanche dogs. Aren't those especially bred for their noses?"

"Mutts can have good noses, too. Imagine if there is a freak avalanche that takes out a school bus, and Hunter and Woody are the ones to save all those innocent children. They'll be famous."

"Stop. First, that's a horrible scenario. Second, Woody and Hunter?"

"I came up with those names at lunch. Hunter for the girl."

They're not terrible names for dogs. Better than Petunia Blum, for sure. "Do I get a say in naming *our* dogs?"

"Perhaps. As long as you don't pick something like Namaste or Green Tea."

I resist the urge to push him into the lake. "Those aren't dog names."

"Okay, give it your best effort." He brushes the back of his hand against mine. I repeat the gesture to him, and he responds by interlacing our fingers.

"Woody makes me think of erections."

"No more Woody."

"Hunter is okay, but for a boy, not a girl."

He swings our hands together. "One down, one to go."

As the path narrows, we're forced to walk single file. He steps ahead of me and I trail behind him.

"Flower and plant names are out." I stumble slightly over a small rock.

He checks over his shoulder to make sure I'm all right. "Watch out for those pebbles back there. Rocks are dangerous.

Even the small ones could take us both out."

"You're never going to live that down."

He twists his head and I can see his grin. "I'm sure you'll remind me when I'm old and forgetful."

My heart skips a beat in its rhythm at the thought of growing old with him. "Dogs can live ten or fifteen years. You'll be stuck with me for at least another decade."

He squeezes my hand. "Then we better settle on names."

My mind blanks as I try to think of a proper name for a girl dog.

"How about Aspen ski runs? Dipsey Doodle? Short Snort?"

I laugh. "I'm not owning a dog named Short Snort. Or anything with Dump as part of the name."

"You're really narrowing your options."

Light-bulb moment. "How about Nell?"

He stops and I bump into his side. "Perfect. Little Nell."

He looks so happy with my suggestion I stretch up on my tiptoes to kiss his cheek. His beard teases and tickles when I press my lips against his skin.

A chuckle turns into a moan-growl before he sweeps his arm around me, pulling me against his side. As I inhale in surprise, he brushes his lips against mine.

I kiss him back at the same time I wrap my arms around his neck.

Tightening his arm against my back and shifting his weight to his good leg, his arm holding the cane curves around my lower back, anchoring me to him.

My chest presses against the hard planes and ridges of his torso. I want to release his hair from the bun and run my fingers through his waves.

So I do. Threading my fingers into his hair, I gently pull out the hair tie. I twist it on my own wrist. When I scratch his scalp, he groans into my mouth like a lion. No, too golden. He's a panther. All sleek strength and dark grace.

He rolls his hips and lust sparks in my blood from the point of contact. I lower my hands, tracing the outline of triceps and biceps before moving to his pecs. Wiggling my arms under his, I'm able to explore his back muscles. My palms travel down his spine until I reach the glory of his ass. Without care to who could come down this trail and see us making out, I squeeze. He flexes and his hardness presses into my stomach.

This time I'm the one moaning. Breathless, I reluctantly slow our kiss by sucking on his bottom lip before placing a small peck on the corner of his mouth, and pulling away.

His chest rises and falls against mine as he collects his breath. A lack of oxygen doesn't stop him from kissing my jaw, my neck, and gently sucking on the place where my shoulder begins.

A clatter of metal on rocks confuses me. I pull away slightly and open my eyes. He stares back at me with hooded lids and slowly blinks.

"I dropped my cane."

"Ah." Neither of us moves.

He kisses me again, slipping his tongue between my lips. I taste the salt and citrus from his margarita.

"You're spicy," he whispers an inch from my mouth.

"I was thinking you're salty." I open my eyes.

He licks his own bottom lip. "You're right."

"We're making out in the middle of a hiking trail."

He opens his eyes wider and twists around to scan the trail. "I don't think the ducks are minding. Or the marmot squeaking at us from the grove of Aspens."

The squeals of small children break the silence. From the direction of the parking lot comes a small army of tiny invaders.

"Should we stand our ground against them?" He steps back

so he's no longer pressed against me and discreetly rearranges himself.

"We're severely outnumbered." I count at least fifteen backpack sporting kids racing around the trailhead.

"Maybe if their chaperones spy us performing adult acts, they'll realize they've come at the wrong time and leave."

I giggle at his crazy words. "We'll be arrested. It's the middle of the afternoon and US Forest land."

"I could be deported!" He reaches down and grabs his cane. Tugging my hand, he tries to pull me toward the parking lot. "Run!"

I gape at him.

"I'm joking." He brushes a lock of my hair behind my ear. "But I'm disappointed you didn't panic at the thought of losing me."

"It's shock. You can't say those things."

"The government doesn't care if I'm making out in a park. At least I don't think they'd bother to prosecute me."

We walk slowly back to the car, encountering the school field trip near the information kiosk.

"Good afternoon," he says to the group. "Be careful of the bears."

A short girl with blond curls screams and hugs the legs of one of the adults.

"Thanks for the head's up," the chaperone says.

"We didn't see any bears," I whisper.

"Always good to be careful of bears. I've gifted Goldilocks back there with solid life advice."

We manage to keep our hands to ourselves and our clothes on during the short drive back to our condos.

However, the second we're standing at the front door, Lee leans in close and whispers, "Let's finish what we started."

I can only nod as I follow him inside his place.

With a deep inhale, I try to steady my racing heart. Whatever fire he ignited in me on the mountain still burns. When he brushes his hand down my arm and reclaims my hand, I lean into him, resting my head against his chest.

We've crossed a line, but kissing is nothing compared to getting naked together. Seeing him naked will change everything. *What happens if it's terrible? If I'm terrible? What if he isn't turned on by naked me?*

"Lee . . ."

FIFTEEN

STAN

SAGE IS HESITATING and shutting down.

Tension tightens her shoulders and she won't make eye contact.

"Lee . . ." My preferred name on her lips is a splash of cold water, not the sexy whisper I crave.

Lifting her chin, I make her look at me.

"We'll figure it out," I reassure her.

"What if . . ."

"Don't fall into the hypothetical pit. Be with me in the moment. Here." I press her hand to my chest.

Her fingers flex against my pec. I wonder if she can feel my heart banging against her touch. "Are you sure?"

"Never been more certain in my life. Nothing you say is going to change my mind. I don't care about anything right now other than being naked with you, being inside of you. Everything else we can figure out later."

"But . . ."

"No. Stop thinking. Feel."

I slide my tongue along the curve of her ear and she shivers.

My teeth sink into the tender flesh with gentle pressure.

A sound escapes her. A moan. I pause. If she's telling me no, I'll listen. I would never force myself on a woman. Her hands tighten in my shirt and begin to lift it up.

My breath warming the trail of kisses I left on her neck, I whisper close to her ear, "We can stop at any time. You're in charge. Say the word, and it ends."

She cups my cheek and reclaims my mouth, invading it with a sweep of her tongue. Her mouth tastes of citrus, spice, and something uniquely Sage. It's intoxicating.

I take over again, angling her head to go deeper. I can't get enough of her; roaming my fingers down her neck, caressing her shoulders and upper arms before letting my hands drift over her breasts. They're small, but round and full. I gently cup them. My palms covering them entirely, I feel her nipples tighten beneath my touch.

She moans into my mouth and scrapes her fingers along my scalp. I love the feel of her nails against my skin. Leaning forward, I encourage her to keep doing it.

Not breaking our kiss, I move us to the couch. My knee settles between her thighs and I have to resist grinding against her hip.

I've been keeping her at a distance for so long, the last thing I want is to move too fast and spook her. The entire silly smoothie "bet" presented itself and I knew I could use it to get closer to her. Closer but keep it casual.

Maintain our boundaries as friends.

In other words, protect myself from getting too emotionally invested.

Or so I told myself.

I knew I'd failed the day in her kitchen when we knocked heads and she asked me to kiss it better. The moment my lips touched her skin was the moment I waved the white flag, and surrendered.

Now she's kissing me and sucking on my tongue while her hands tug at my hair in the most amazing, almost painful way. The sensation travels down my spine and straight to my cock.

More important than relieving the building pressure is giving her pleasure. I need to make her come. I'll use everything I've got to push her over the edge.

After unzipping and removing her fleece, I squeeze one nipple with my fingers. I drag my other hand down her stomach. Her skin feels warm and soft. She gasps when I tuck a single finger under the band of her shorts. Her muscles tighten and flex beneath my hand.

I pull far enough from her mouth to whisper, "Relax. I want to make you feel good."

She blinks open her eyes and stares into mine. "I . . . I want to make you feel good, too."

"You do, *liefie*. You already make me feel so good." I sneak my hand into her shorts and beneath her underwear to explore her. More soft, warm skin greets me. I kiss her nipple through the thin cotton before moving it out of my way.

I slide two fingers inside of her with ease. She's so turned on and ready for me.

"You want this?" I glance up to find her staring at me, a small smile playing on her lips.

With a nod, she encourages me.

"Tell me what you want." I circle a finger around her clit and her hips lift off the couch.

"You."

"You have me." I tweak her nipple. "What else do you want?"

"This." She palms me. I feel her warm hand reach inside my pants, pushing them out of the way. "Can I touch you?"

I nod.

She finds the wet spot at the tip and traces the ridge. When she grips me, I inhale sharply.

"Too tight?" She loosens her hold, which doesn't quite encircle me.

"No, it's been a while. Give me a minute."

Her hand feels worlds apart from my own, the only source of pleasure I've had in . . . I pause to think. Months. Since before my unfortunate encounter with the rock.

I place my hand over hers and guide her into a rhythm matching the one my other hand is using on her.

She's a quick learner. I return my hand to her breast as I lean forward to kiss her again, letting my tongue tangle with hers. With my eyes closed, I'm more in tune with her sounds and the small reactions of her body to my touch.

"I want to make you come," I whisper against her lips.

I fucking love exploring her body like this. Figuring out what she likes and how she reacts is an incredible feeling. Knowing it's my touch and my kiss causing the soft moans, trembles, and breathy pants turns me on more than anything.

Her hand releases me to grip my bicep. As I feel her tighten around my fingers, I circle my thumb and focus my pressure inside her.

I open my eyes to memorize how she looks as she breaks apart. The flush of pink from her nipples up to her jaw, and the shallow rise of her ribs as she breathes before holding her breath when she is swept away.

I did this.

I gave this angel wings.

She floats down from the high and stills my fingers with her hand. Her lips curve into a soft smile when she pulls me close.

I brush my lips along hers before she slips her tongue into

my mouth.

"Thank you," I whisper.

"Shouldn't I be thanking you?" Her words are breathy and sated.

"No."

She blinks open her eyes. "No?"

I shake my head, rubbing my nose against hers. "I love giving you pleasure. You've given me something pure, something precious."

A small line appears between her eyes. I realize how my words sound.

"I'm not talking about your virginity."

Surprise then amusement flashes behind her eyes before she giggles.

"I'm trying to have a moment here, do you mind?" I grin down at her, shaking as I try not to join her in laughing at myself. My erection brushes against her thigh. "Sorry."

She takes me in her hand again. "Why are you apologizing?"

"Nothing like having a moment, then being laughed at and poking my erection into your thigh like a pest."

With a squeeze of her hand, I stop talking.

"I think we should finish this in bed."

"Are you sure?" She could lead me anywhere with her hand on my cock.

"Sage orgasms, one. Stan orgasms, zero. Don't you want to even the score?"

"It's not a competition—"

This time she's the one who uses a kiss to silence the conversation.

SIXTEEN

SAGE

MY HAND WRAPS around Lee and I basically pull him down the hall to his bedroom by his penis.

Talk about caveman behavior.

Or in this case, cavewoman.

I'm not dragging him. He follows me willingly with one hand on my ass as I try to walk backward without running into a wall. Again.

"You should be steering us," I whisper against his mouth. "You're facing forward and can see where we're going."

"Sorry, *liefie*, my mind's more than a little preoccupied by your hand on me right now." He squeezes my cheek.

How we manage to propel ourselves forward is a mystery. His pants hang below his hips. We're like two turtles in one shell, glued together in the middle, but with an extra set of legs attempting to coordinate and walk. When I feel the mattress at the back of my legs, I give up the fight and fall backward, releasing Lee.

He quickly climbs on top of me, but keeps most of his weight braced on his elbows. We resume kissing and soon he switches our positions, pulling me on top of him.

I shift to straddle him, settling my knees on either side of his hips. This position allows me to explore his chest. I push his shirt up, giving me access to his skin. He takes the hint and curls up. Reaching behind his neck, he yanks it off and tosses it over my head to the floor.

"Yours next." He kisses my neck in his upright position. His hands tug on my long sleeve T-shirt. Cool air tickles my skin as he lifts it up. I raise my arms to help him. "This too."

His nose nuzzles the swell of my breasts above my pale pink bra. The laundry gods were smiling upon me this morning when I managed to coordinate my underwear and bra. I feel his fingers trace up my spine until he reaches my bra. With a quick flick of his hand, he smoothly undoes the clasp.

"Let go," he whispers, kissing my breast.

I'm still holding the cups against my skin.

"Trust me."

I release my hands and exhale.

"Look at me." His voice is soft, but commanding.

I obey, feeling the fabric slide down my arms while I stare into his vulnerable beautiful eyes. He keeps his focus on my face, a soft, sweet smile tilting up his lips.

"Beautiful." He hasn't looked anywhere but my face.

I lift my hands to cup his jaw, softly scratching his beard. He tilts his head to lean into my touch. With his eyes closed, he gives me permission to explore the architecture of his face and shoulders. I trace along the planes of his cheekbones and nose before smoothing my thumbs over his dark brows. His long lashes create shadows below his eyes.

"Beautiful." I echo his words.

He accepts my compliment with a throaty chuckle, gripping my hips and thrusting against me.

"That's from your touch. You do this to me." I feel how hard and long he is. The only thing separating us now are my shorts and underwear. I rise on my knees to remove them. My momentary shyness from earlier dissipates.

Lee shoves his jeans down and they get caught on his boot. "I forgot something."

I stand to undo the Velcro on his boot. "Are you okay with it off?"

"I am. I promise."

I set the boot on the floor.

He slides to the edge of the bed and pulls me closer. "Let me help."

I feel his rough hands smooth over my hips as he rids me of the last of my clothing. My skin pebbles in the wake of his touch. I shiver, but not from the cold.

He kisses my stomach and cups my bottom.

I smooth my hands over and through his hair, resisting the urge to pull it.

"Are you steering?" He smiles against my skin and kisses above my bellybutton.

I giggle. "Mind reader."

A gentle pressure on my hip shifts me to the right. "Lie down."

I crawl up the bed and rest my head on the pillows.

He begins at my ankles, kissing up my legs to the tops of my thighs.

The shy feeling returns. I haven't showered since this morning. The thought makes me press my legs together.

Lee notices. "What's wrong? I promise to make you feel amazing."

Do I lie and say I'm not that into it?

And miss out on living out one of my fantasies?

"I . . . um . . ."

He quirks his eyebrow, his thumbs skimming my inner thighs, willing them to open.

"Ishoweredthismorningbutit'sbeenalongdayandI'mnotso . . . fresh."

"The only part of that I understood is fresh." Understanding lights up his eyes. "Oh."

I still his hands. Clearly, I've ruined the moment.

He surprises me when he shrugs and kisses across to each hip. Never taking his eyes off of mine, he gives me a sly smile and inhales.

He smirks at my gasp and gently pushes his hands between my thighs.

This time when I clench my legs together, it's to calm the building need to grind against something for friction. Preferably his beard and tongue.

He drags his tongue from my navel down, farther down until my body responds and opens for him.

The long fingers I've admired for years now softly explore me, pressing against my most sensitive spots and learning my body's reaction. He sucks and licks, bringing me closer and closer to the edge before he slows his pace and lightens the pressure.

Soon I'm ready to beg him for another release.

I grab his hair and pull, holding his mouth against me as I buck my hips, grasping for that elusive final element to unlocking bliss.

Lee's low laugh sends a vibration over my skin. The new sensation pushes me closer. I tug his hair again, hinting I need more. He responds by reaching up and pinching one of my nipples. Hard. The sudden jolt of pain shocks me and my body responds with a wave of pleasure unlike anything I've ever experienced before. My orgasm takes over, causing me to tremble and moan in breathy pants.

He squeezes again, curling his fingers and I'm lost.

I loosen my grip in his hair and flop back into the pillows. When he kisses my inner thigh, I buck off the bed. Everything feels too sensitive, too much.

Another kiss to my tender nipple and I shiver.

I feel his lips curl into a grin when he reaches my collarbone, leaving a wet kiss along the ridge.

I manage to pry open my eyes to see him smirking down at me.

I'm too blissed out to come up with any witty response.

His erection brushes against my hip, a reminder he still hasn't come.

"Sage, two. Lee, zero," I mumble.

"Let's remedy that, shall we?" He leans over me to reach his nightstand. He places the corner of the foil package in his mouth to tear it with his teeth. Condoms aren't sexy, but watching Lee roll one onto himself is beyond hot.

I guide him to me before letting him take over.

Again, he stares into my eyes as he brushes the tip across my wet skin, dipping into my entrance before teasing me more.

I frown at him and he pauses.

"What's wrong?"

"Stop teasing me."

"Oh, *liefie*. I'm torturing myself more than anything." The furrow between his brows reveals his concentration on controlling this moment.

"Why?"

"Because I've been waiting for this moment for a long time. We'll never have another first time."

His words melt me. Never another first time for us as a couple or in our lives? Forever?

I tilt my hips and he slips farther in, but it's not enough. He stills and inhales. Lifting his hand, he runs a knuckle over my cheek before capturing my mouth with his.

While kissing me, he thrusts, slowly entering me. I love feeling my body adjust to the size of him, stretching and relaxing before he's finally all the way inside.

Wrapping my legs around his hips, I attempt to encourage him to move.

"Are you going to pull my hair again?" He chuckles against my lips. "I'm not a horse. You can't tell me to giddy-up and go."

His words make me giggle. I take them as a challenge and grab a section of hair at his nape. Not steering. I love the sound he makes when I tug. If panthers growl, they probably sound like him.

Pinning my arms above my head, he increases his pace. The headboard knocks against the wall with his thrusts. I grin up at him, thinking how we share a wall and I've never heard his headboard thump.

I pull his head down to kiss him, sliding my tongue against his while trying not to smile. His hand cups my breast and squeezes as he speeds up, his rhythm faltering. When he stills, I open my eyes to watch his face shatter into bliss.

I love how unguarded he is with his eyes closed and his mouth open.

He's beautiful and never more so in this moment.

SEVENTEEN

STAN

I FIGHT MY instinct to pull away from Sage now that we've had sex.

Incredible sex.

None of the awkward moments of being naked in front of a stranger, not knowing her last name or trying to avoid small talk. Or talking at all.

With Sage, I know all the little details about her. Her favorite color. Her favorite food. What she looks like right out of the shower and first thing in the morning. How she takes her tea because she only drinks coffee in the morning.

I never realized how deeply she's penetrated my world.

Focused on not getting close to her, not letting her in, I missed the ways she snuck inside through my cracks and weak spots.

She's still asleep next to me. I listen to her even breathing while I lie awake, my brain running wild with hypotheticals and worst case scenarios.

I can't fuck this up. Not with Sage. All the reasons why I stayed away from her are still valid. Instead of counting sheep, I list them in my head. Emotions make life messy. I'm not ready for a serious relationship. Women are distractions, not the goal. I need to focus on rugby while I can still compete.

As I run through my list, I hear my father's voice.

He's drilled this thinking into my head since fifteen. Every single truth I've been telling myself is nothing more than an excuse, a defense mechanism.

A lie.

No better way to get clarity than standing in freezing cold water holding a pole, pretending to fly fish.

For generations men have gone to lakes, rivers, seas, and oceans to stare out at the water and think. We call it fishing because as men, we're not supposed to be deep emotional thinkers and have introspection on our lives.

Sometimes we even have fish to show for a day spent sitting around not doing much.

I'm down valley standing in the Roaring Fork River with numb feet and two nimrods to keep me company. It's our annual pre-Fourth of July mankend. A weekend of fly-fishing, eating anything we can catch, drinking beer and sitting around a campfire telling tall tales.

Or arguing about rugby.

Sometimes the talk turns to women. That's the tall tales part of the night.

The hot women who we allegedly shagged. Or the even hotter ones who somehow got away.

I don't feel like participating much this year.

When the conversation turns to me, I answer a few questions about Sage and my relationship as broadly and vaguely as possible. I'd rather be home and spending the weekend with her. I can't and don't say this out loud to the guys.

It's been four days since I woke up with Sage in my bed. Four days of busy work schedules and prepping for this trip. We haven't had the chance to hang out. Or talked more than a passing "hey" outside our condos.

Me wanting to talk about my feelings is a sign of the apocalypse. Or the reality I'm falling in love with my best friend.

Honestly, it wasn't awkward the next morning. She left early for a class. I walked her to the door and kissed her forehead. Told her how beautiful she is.

I might be freaking out a little, but in a good way. I almost cancelled this weekend to spend it with her, but she's busy with the start of ballet camp. We'll see each other in a few days at the big party for the Fourth of July.

The guys keep giving me shit for gaming the list. Let them. Real or fake, all they need to know about what goes on between Sage and me is that we're dating.

Landon overshares about Tess and caps it off by sharing she dumped him. Of course she did. Easley is still after Chelsea the massage therapist despite asking for a happy ending after their first date. He's persistent; I'll give him that.

I keep the conversation focused on my return to the team and the match next week.

I finally have the go ahead from both my doctor and trainer.

I'm back in the game.

Life is returning to normal.

Except the new situation with Sage.

How long can we be in a fake relationship when my feelings are real?

I've put us in this box and now I need to figure a way out.

EIGHTEEN

SAGE

LEE STANDS A few feet away, holding a fresh pint glass of beer in his hand. In a blue and white striped rugby shirt, he looks like the athlete he is, but something about him is different.

He's a little tanner than when I saw him last week. Probably from the fishing trip and playing rugby again. The beard is still there. It's not longer or shaggier. I'm guessing he had it professionally groomed after being a mountain man with the guys. Damn I've missed him. Seven days since Lee and I made love, but it feels like months since I've been alone with him.

When he turns to the side, I see his full profile.

That's when it hits me.

I gasp.

Loudly.

An older couple immediately in front of me stares. Probably trying to decipher if I'm crazy, drunk, or in some sort of trouble.

"Excuse me." I sidle around them.

"Is everything all right, dear?" the elegant woman in a stars and stripes sweater asks.

"Fine, fine. Had a bit of a shock. Nothing another glass of

champagne won't fix."

"Champagne can cure a myriad of life's woes." She raises her glass in a salute.

I grab a fresh one off the bar and clink glasses with her. When I turn to find Lee, he's disappeared.

Standing on my tiptoes, I search the enormous white tent. The crowd looks like a lawn full of American flags. Normally, I'd be looking for his bun.

But it's gone.

Stan the Man Bun has cut off his knot. No more easy to spot knot.

Ironically, I can immediately count four other men in the crowd with buns of various girths and heights. Every size, shape, and color bun. Tiny thumb size nubs. Ones that look enhanced and too perfect. Man buns abound in beer garden.

It's bunpalooza here at the Aspen Fourth of July concert. Perhaps I've been wrong about the trend being over. I'd even say it's reached a crescendo.

I giggle at my music joke even though I didn't say it out loud.

A waiter stops with a tray of mini caprese salad bites. I take one and a napkin. Intended to be a perfect one-bite size, I stuff the cherry tomato and boccatini into my mouth.

Must be for a bigger mouth than mine. I cover my chewing with one hand holding the napkin.

"You look lovely tonight," a familiar voice compliments me from behind.

I finish chomping and take sip of my bubbly.

"Hello, Landon. Are you saying my ass looks lovely in these white jeans?" He's wearing a yellow sweater, clearly having missed the red, white, and blue theme on the invitation.

"Oh, Sage. Always so funny." He doesn't answer my question, which is an answer in and of itself. Guilty.

"I get paid by the laughs."

He stares at me.

"Are you here for the concert?" It's a dumb question. Why else would he be here.

"I couldn't tell you who is playing what tonight. I crashed for the free food and open bar."

Classy. "Seems like a lot of effort for some free eats."

He shrugs. "Nothing really gets started until after the fireworks, so I figured I might as well grab some free booze and grub."

"Beef sliders?" another waiter asks, extending his tray in front of us.

"Oh, yeah. Load me up." Landon takes a napkin and stacks four mini-burgers on it while the waiter and I watch. "Aren't you going to have any, Sage?"

"I didn't want to lose a finger while you took yours." I give the waiter an empathetic smile. "At least he saves you from making a full circuit of the tent."

The waiter smiles, but doesn't comment on the rude behavior of one of the evening's guests. Normally I know more of the catering staff at these events than the guests, but he's unfamiliar to me. Probably a college kid here for the summer. He wanders away with a mostly empty tray.

"You know . . ." I start to scold Landon, but stop myself. He's not my monkey and I don't want to be part of his circus.

"Pork bun?" another waiter suggests.

"She doesn't like buns." Lee's deep voice comes from over my shoulder. "Don't even get her started on man buns. The hair kind. Not the arse ones."

The waiter turns away and Landon trails after him, grabbing more food for his napkin picnic.

I whisper over my shoulder, "You said arse to the young

cater waiter. Don't sexually harass the staff, please."

Lee presses his lips against my cheek. Stepping around me, he runs a hand through his hair. Still long enough to fall into his eyes, but no longer bun-able. "Well?"

"I really do like pork buns. I'm sad you frightened away the waiter."

"Always so stubborn." He brushes the back of his hand down my arm, reminding me what a single touch from him can do to my body. I check to make sure my clothes haven't incinerated.

"You cut your hair."

"I did." The expression in his eyes is vulnerable, silently asking me what I think.

"I love it." I touch the soft locks at the top.

"Good," he says with a nod. "My best friend hated it. I love to make her happy. Nothing gives me more pleasure."

The double meaning of his words hangs between us.

I respond with my own cryptic comment. "You should listen to this friend more often."

"I should." His gaze holds mine.

Overwhelmed by his hotness factor doubling without the bun, I awkwardly change the subject.

"Is the rugby club co-sponsoring the event tonight? Landon was raiding the catering trays like it's his last meal."

A low grumble of disapproval rumbles in his chest. "Figures. He's a caveman. We're supposed to be here promoting the rugby fest in the fall. You know how the old guys love to brag about still playing rugby. Badge of honor and all."

"One of these days, you'll be one of those old coots complaining about your knees and still giving the other guys hell on the pitch."

He grins. "Naturally."

"Speaking of complaining about things, how's the ankle?"

Gone are his cane and the boot, the last signs of his injury.

"Seems fine. It's been eight weeks since the break. My physical therapist is letting me train and play partial games soon." He frowns and his bottom lip pouts like a little boy.

"How many matches have you missed?"

"Five and counting. My trainer keeps saying next week. He's been telling me next week for almost a month now."

"It's only early July."

"I haven't seriously trained since May. Eight weeks. Now the season is half over."

"My glass is half empty, but you don't see me complaining." I hold up my nearly empty champagne flute.

A waiter appears with a tray of full glasses.

"Thank you." I swap out my glass for a fresh one. "See?"

"What?" An adorable crease appears between his brows.

I want to smooth it out and whisper everything will be fine. My fingers tingle in anticipation of touching his skin. With a sigh, I remind myself what a bad idea it is to play with fire.

"The champagne is a metaphor for life. When you think things are terrible and horrible, a fresh perspective can change everything. Or in this case, a full glass."

"I was thinking more like the cheap ones give you regret in the morning followed by a killer headache."

"Now you sound like you're talking about women."

"Could be." His intense stare ruffles me. I know he's not talking about me, but the reminder of his exploits knots my stomach.

NINETEEN

STAN

A FANCY PARTY on the Fourth of July feels un-American. We should be gathered around a grill or open fire, wearing shorts and tekkies, toasting weenies and drinking beers from cans. A proper South African braai would feel more patriotic.

My reflex is to tighten my bun or pull my hair out and redo it. It's a nervous habit I've had for years. Only now, it's too short to do anything but run my fingers through it, pushing it off of my forehead.

The decision was spontaneous when we got back to town after the mankend. I needed a beard trim and while sitting in the chair, told Charlie the barber to add a haircut.

I feel exposed.

I'm standing in a tent full of other men wearing red, white and blue surrounded by a sea of women dressed as star-covered flags. Standing amid them is Sage. In her simple blue top and white jeans, she's unaware she's the most beautiful creature among mere mortals.

Landon chats her up while stuffing food into his napkin like a squirrel hoarding nuts for winter.

I weave along the perimeter of the tent, keeping out of her line of sight, wanting to surprise her. From behind, I notice her hair is now a rich blue on the ends, coordinating with her outfit. Her shirt exposes her shoulders and the way her jeans cling to the curve of her ass reminds me of having her naked in my bed.

I hope to have a lot more Sage soon.

Sage brushes her fingers through my shorter hair. I lean into her touch, letting it ground me. I need the reminder of our connection's strength.

"You like it?" I ask again, feeling oddly insecure and needy of her approval.

"I love it. Aren't you worried about being like Samson? What if all your magical powers were in your bun?" Her smile is playful, teasing.

"I'll have to borrow yours, Delilah." I pull a blue lock of hair through my fingers.

"You're so cheesy." Her words fade into giggling.

"Says the girl comparing my bun to some Old Testament dude."

Her laughter is contagious and soon we're both laughing over nothing.

"Aren't the two of you cozy?" Tess's voice breaks our bubble. "I guess the rumors are true."

Sage stills and goes silent.

"Hello, Tess." I rest my hand on Sage's shoulder, claiming her.

"What rumors?" Sage asks.

Tess smirks. It's not a good look on her. "You haven't heard? Everyone's talking about you two. How Lee put you on the off-limits list so he could fuck you without any competition."

"Excuse me?" Sage's voice rises.

I shrug off Tess's rude comment. "All part of my mastermind plan."

"Your plan?" Sage doesn't look amused. "You had a plan to fuck me?"

Is she joking? Her expression looks deadly, but I can't tell if it's an act for Tess.

I laugh nervously. I don't recognize the sound. "I had a plan to date you."

Tess snorts. "That's not what the guys are saying."

"Since when do they know anything about my life?" I realize I'm going to have to set Landon and Easley straight. My don't ask, don't tell policy is exploding around me.

"We haven't exactly dated," Sage says softly. Her face reveals confusion and insecurity. I never want her to doubt herself around me.

"I'd never leave the house if I was the one screwing Lee." Tess somehow makes a wink dirty.

Sage bristles beside me. I enclose her hand in mine, but she doesn't return the pressure.

"We're not just fucking." I squeeze Sage's hand, wanting to reassure her we're more. "We've been friends, close friends a long time."

"Ah, so you do admit to being friends with benefits?" Tess claps her hands. "I knew it. Landon swears it's all an act. If I didn't know better, I'd say he's jealous."

"Maybe it is? Maybe nothing is real." Sage crosses her arms, leaving my hand in mid-air.

I stuff my fingers into my back pocket. "Maybe we're friends having a laugh."

"Well, that's a waste." Tess clucks her tongue like a judgmental chicken.

I lean close to Sage's ear to whisper, "Can we discuss this without an audience? I need to talk to you. I think it's time for this fake relationship to end."

Fireworks explode over the top of Aspen Mountain. Booms echo around the valley, bouncing off the rocks and hills. Conversation becomes impossible.

Sage pulls out her phone and begins tapping the screen, turning her back to the colorful display.

"Sage?" I brush her shoulder.

"Give me a moment." She walks away. "I need to focus on this."

What the hell just happened?

Sage has gone from sweet smiles and flirting with me, to cold as a January night in the mountains.

I'm not saying she's frigid, but ice wouldn't melt in her mouth right now.

She winds a path across the crowded space, heading for the bar. Her focus is still on her phone.

I let her go.

As I stare at the spot where she disappeared, I become aware I'm now staring at a beautiful woman in a bright red dress. Slightly older, and very well maintained, she raises her champagne flute in my direction.

I'm tempted to turn around to see if she means me, but from the sly smile on her unnaturally plump lips, I have no doubt I'm the one.

When I don't respond, her lips form a frown and she spins on her expensive heel. A giant rock flashes on her left hand.

Definitely, not even remotely, not interested.

I glance at my watch, a gift from my father. When I realized he'd rather buy my love and loyalty than earn it, or reciprocate it, I asked for the vintage Rolex as a birthday gift.

The card that accompanied it was generic and the signature of "Love, Dad" wasn't in my father's writing.

I love the watch, even if it represents the sad reality of my relationship with my father. Or maybe because it's a good reminder how money trumps all and emotions should be avoided, or at the very minimum, controlled.

I stand alone while everyone oohs and ahhs over the fireworks lighting up the sky. I've never understood the fascination. Fireworks are loud and it's always the same show, with slight variations. Whiz. Explosion. Boom. Ooh. Repeat for far too long.

When the frequency and size of the explosions reach a peak, I search the party for Sage.

She's gone.

She left without saying good-bye.

I head home and knock on her door. The lights are off and she doesn't answer. I could use my key, but if she needs time and space, I'll give it to her tonight.

I'll bring coffee over in the morning and tell her how I'm feeling without fighting with fireworks to be heard.

TWENTY

SAGE

I CATCH A cab from O'Hare straight to the hospital.

I text Lee a short message:

In Chicago.

Rose is having the baby.

I'm not sure what else to say after last night.

He certainly seemed pleased with himself over our fake relationship working so well for him. But then he said we're friends, only friends, and told me the fake relationship needed to end. He promised we'd chat today or soon. Have a good laugh about it all.

At least that's what I think he meant. With the fireworks going off and my phone lighting up with texts from Rose, I only half paid attention.

Rose, who is always so perfectly scheduled and organized, started having contractions in the wee hours of today, two weeks early.

Now I'm in a cab, stuck in traffic, worried about my sister, tired, and more confused by Lee than ever.

My parents are flying in from the Hamptons in a few hours. To say my mother is annoyed with the thought of missing the birth of her first grandchild is the understatement of the century. She convinced my father to hire a helicopter to take them into the city to catch the earliest flight possible.

Blums do not like to be frivolous. Or surprised.

My phone chirps with a text from Archie with an update on Rose. Her labor seems to have stalled. They're monitoring the situation.

I note he didn't do a group text and forward it to my mother. She's thirty-five thousand feet in the air, but will be mad if she's not kept in the loop.

The cab drops me off outside Northwestern Memorial and I lug my suitcase inside. I have no idea how long I'll be here for, so I overpacked all my clothes. At least the clean ones. I was in such a rush to leave before dawn this morning; I'm wearing the same yoga pants I slept in.

I text Archie for their room number and head upstairs.

"Sis!" Rose is happily munching away on ice chips when I walk into her private room.

"Shouldn't you be cursing Archie and screaming obscenities right about now?"

"My contractions stopped."

I eye Archie with concern. His normally perfectly pressed chinos are wrinkled, as is his navy polo shirt. He has ginger stubble and his auburn curls are in need of a trim.

"It's nothing to be too worried about. She's early and this can happen." He smiles and it's genuine.

I sit on Rose's bed and listen to the beeping of her monitors. A faster flutter comes from the baby monitor strapped to her enormous belly.

"Wow. You got huge." I cringe, waiting for her to yell at me.

Scowling, she pets her protruding midsection. "I'm a whale. Look at my cankles."

I stare at the space where her ankles used to be. "It looks like your calves ate your ankles and your feet are next."

We laugh and catch up while nurses come in and randomly check her. One snaps on a pair of gloves and pulls out the stirrups. It's my cue to check out the view from the window.

The doctor appears to reassure Rose this happens all the time. Given it's weeks before her due date, she's to not come back until her contractions are consistently four minutes apart. A nurse has Archie fill out some discharge paperwork as we pack up Rose's things under a cloud of disappointment.

I rub her shoulder in the elevator. "Now we can hang out together before you turn into a dairy cow."

Our humor hasn't matured one bit since we were kids. She snorts and gives me a watery smile. "I'm so over being pregnant. Whoever decided I should be a million months pregnant in July in Chicago is evil."

"You have no one to blame but yourself. And Archie." I give my favorite brother-in-law a sympathetic smile.

"Is it too late to call off Mom and Dad?" Rose asks.

"Oh, crap." I check their flight on my phone. Mom hasn't texted yet, so they must still be midair. "They're en route."

"We should stop by Giordino's and grab something to go. I'm starved. All I've eaten today are those damn ice chips."

"Hangry woman coming through," I shout when the elevator doors open. Archie pushes Rose's wheelchair ahead of me. My sister laughs and it's a relief she's not crying.

Give her five minutes and that might change.

Telling them I'll be right back, I dash into the gift shop. The candy selection is impressive for a place concerned about people's health. I toss an armful on the counter and pay.

Rose sits by the doors when I return. I place the bag in her lap. "I raided candyland for you. I don't want to ride with you if you're pregnant *and* hangry. You might kill Archie with your bare hands and super-human mom strength."

She bites into a Snickers bar without removing the wrapping.

"Settle down, Cujo." I carefully extract the chocolate from her gnashing teeth and unwrap it.

Big, heavy tears slide down her face as she chews. "I really want to be a mom."

"I know. And you will be. You don't really have a choice at this point. Just not today. We'll load you up with lots of spicy food and beer, then send you upstairs to screw your husband's brains out. Sound good?"

She nods and smiles a chocolaty grin.

"Hold that for a second." I snap a pic with my phone. "We're putting this one in the baby album."

She tries to steal my phone when she sees the hideous picture. "I will kill you if you don't delete that right now."

Her scary mom voice is impressive given she's not an actual mother yet.

My life is saved by Archie and his family sedan pulling up to the curb. I push Rose's wheelchair through the doors. While Archie helps lift her and her cankles out of the chair, I toss my bag in the backseat and climb in.

Mom and Dad crowd Rose's kitchen looking like a couple in a lifestyle magazine ad for the Hamptons. Both are golden tan, but not too dark, from playing tennis. Dad's wearing his uniform of chinos and a blue linen shirt. He dresses like Ina Garten, but I'll never tell him that. Mom's rocking one of her signature Lilly Pulitzer dress, a matching pink cardigan, and Jack Rogers sandals aka the same summer outfit she's worn all my life.

They missed us at the hospital because Mom didn't check her texts.

Or I forgot to hit send on the one alerting them of the false alarm.

Mom fusses around the space, pulling out plates from the dishwasher and opening drawers in search of silverware. "We're going to have to reorganize your entire kitchen. Nothing is in the right place."

Rose and I make eye contact.

"Hannah, it's Rose's house. Let her organize it how she likes." Dad's soothing tone calms Mom. Sometimes when I close my eyes, I can imagine him with the ponytail he sported in college. His receding hairline probably misses those hair glory days.

"But how she likes is wrong. Housewares are our life. She should know how to properly arrange a kitchen." With a sigh, she resigns herself. "I'll reorganize it correctly while you're in the hospital recovering from childbirth."

"Mom! Seriously?" Rose huffs from her sofa nest.

"Honey." Dad leans in for a kiss. I turn away when I see Mom's hand squeeze his ass through his chinos.

"Okay, you two, no making out in the kitchen," Rose shouts from the sofa. "Can someone bring me something to eat?"

Archie fixes her a plate with an enormous slice of stuffed pizza and a tiny portion of salad. He carries the plate and a shaker of red pepper flakes over to his wife.

"He's such a good man," Mom coos. She brushes a hand over her perfectly blond highlighted bob.

I freeze, knowing what's coming next.

"Sage, you need to find yourself a nice guy like Archie. Maybe one of his fraternity brothers from Northwestern is still single. I'm sure not all of them are married by now. There must be one or two like you."

"Like me how?"

"Late bloomers." Her sympathetic smile feels more than a little passively condescending. Like being passive aggressive, but with more frowning and tsking.

"Mom, don't start in on Sage. For all we know, she's playing the field with a hot rugby player in Aspen," Rose says.

I almost do a spit take with my wine. Rose gives me a wink.

There's no way she knows anything about Lee and me. Or our fake relationship with benefits.

"Oh, I hope not. All those Europeans there looking for a quick fling with an American girl." Mom pats my arm.

"I was thinking more about the super-hot South African guy living next door."

Mom's blue eyes widen in panic. Or excitement. On her it's difficult to tell the difference. "Shaka Zulu! Tell me more."

Okay, we're going with excitement.

"I saw a statue of him in London. Those cheekbones. The abs!" Mom has a dazed look in her eyes.

Dad blanches. "Honey, what are you talking about? Shaka Zulu was a warrior king, not a sex symbol."

Mom gives him her patented disappointed mom face. "I remember the mini-series. We watched it together. There really is a statue of him in Camden Market. Shirtless. He could give Fabio a run for his money."

"Who?" I ask.

Rose snorts from her spot on the sofa. "Mom, Sage isn't living next door to a Zulu warrior. Although he could be on those Harlequin novels at the grocery store."

Mom stares at me, waiting for explanation.

"He's Afrikaans."

"Yes, that's what your sister said."

"I mean, he's white."

"Oh, dear. He's not part of those people who created Apartheid, is he?"

"Given he's only twenty-seven, no. He's too young. Plus, he moved here as a teenager. He's not racist."

Dad nods his head, his frown making his chin wrinkle. "What about his parents?"

I answer, realizing I don't know much about his family. Maybe they are on the wrong side of history. Our family has a long tradition of being pro-Civil Rights and active on social issues. Mom's father even volunteered in the South after he got out of law school. Pretty sure Gertrude and Edith were bra burners during the sixties.

"I don't really know. We're just friends."

Mom and Dad have one of their silent parent conferences. "Just?"

I nod.

"Just is a superfluous word," Dad says. "If you're friends, you say 'he's a friend'. You don't need to add the just, which implies friendship alone is not satisfactory."

Both my parents peer at me. Dad pushes up his glasses. Mom taps her wineglass with the tip of her perfectly french manicured fingernail.

I sip my wine and shrug.

"I see," Mom whispers. "Does this 'just a friend' have a name?"

"Lee. Stanley." I say his name like James Bond would introduce himself.

"The Marvel genius?" Dad's clearly amused by his own cleverness.

Chuckling at his own corny joke causes my eyes to roll in

a dormant teenager reflex.

"Who's Stan Lee?" Mom asks.

Dad clutches his heart and dramatically says, "How can the love of my life ask such a question? You are a stranger to me."

Taking my food and glass of wine, I abandon the kitchen for the sanity of the living area. "Scoot over, I need to be with sane people."

Rose settles her resting bitch face on me. "You think I can scoot with an elephant sitting on my bladder?"

"Fine." I squeeze in next to her. She immediately steals my garlic bread.

"Want to tell me what's going on with Mr. South Africa?"

I peek over my shoulder to see Archie in a discussion with the parents.

"Nothing." I take a bite of salad. "Not really."

"Spill," she whispers in the way only an older sister can be threatening and almost silent at the same time. "Now."

I tell her about the kale smoothie, the pretend dating, and the not so pretend kissing. She listens with the garlic bread in one hand, and the other hand over her mouth.

"Only kissing?"

I shake my head and she softly squeals.

Engrossed in the details of my story, I don't hear my mother creep up on us until her perfume engulfs me when the sofa dips behind me. "Just what this time?"

She lovingly wraps her arm around my shoulder in a hug. Or chokehold.

"I'm so out of the loop with you girls these days. Sage, I don't know why you don't spend more time in the Hamps with us during the summer."

"Mom, all those same people are in Aspen in the winter. I need a little break."

"Think how happy your barre clients would be to not have to find someone new. You could probably do all your classes in private homes. Everyone has their own gyms. You could make a fortune during the season!"

She thinks she's being helpful. I know she does. While Dad scoffs at my current job, and never calls it a career, Mom embraces it and tries to push me to a "whole other level" as she puts it.

I definitely didn't inherit the ambition gene from either of them.

"I love the mountains in the summer."

"Of course you do." She toys with the ends of my hair. I dipped them into raspberry Kool-Aid and turned them a robin's egg blue last week. "Sometimes I wonder how you'd have turned out differently if you weren't conceived at the Phish show at the Gorge."

Rose chokes on some garlic bread and I pat her back. "Mom!"

"Oh, sweetheart. It's the truth. Of course we didn't realize it until a few months later."

My sister and I lock eyes. I silently pray she can change the direction this conversation is going before—

"Honey, do you remember where Rose was conceived? Was it in New York? I remember we figured out it was probably during a weekend of wild hotel sex."

"Mom!" both Rose and I shout.

"Honestly, I didn't raise you two to be prudes."

"I still have my copy of Our Bodies, Ourselves you gifted me in fifth grade," Rose says.

"It's so important to be prepared to become a woman and all it encompasses. Including sex."

Rose sweeps her hand over her belly. "Obviously I've had sex, but we don't need to hear where you and Dad fornicated to conceive us."

"I'm merely trying to bond with my daughters." Sighing dejectedly, Mom shifts away from me. "You two have each other to girl talk with whenever you want with your social media and Facetime. I have an iPhone, too, you know."

"Is this about becoming a grandmother?" Rose asks, tilting herself to touch Mom's arm behind me on the sofa. She gets stuck and I have to pull her back to upright.

"I miss my babies." Mom's voice is watery like she's on the brink of tears. "My babies are having babies and don't need their mother anymore."

"That's not true. I don't know what I'm doing. I'm terrified about the baby coming out of me and being responsible for another human." Rose's eyes turn pink along her lids, a sure sign she's about to bawl.

"Oh, sweetheart." Mom lunges forward, trapping me between the two of them.

I hold out my plate and wineglass on either side of Rose.

"Hello? Help?" My voice is muffled because my mouth is pressed against her belly. I'm talking to the baby. Asking for help.

I'm literally being smothered by my mother's love.

"Sorry, Sage." Mom leans away and pats my back.

"Sage is sleeping with her neighbor." Rose covers her mouth but not before the words hang in the room like a bunch of the most awkward balloons ever. We're talking half-deflated penis balloons level of awkward.

"Edith Rose!" I'm the one using both her first and middle name.

"Gertrude Sage." My mother's hand tightens around my bicep. "With the Zulu?"

"No."

Mom frowns.

"He's not a Zulu warrior. We already did this comedy routine in the kitchen."

Rose laughs and laughs. She laughs until she has to lean forward to catch her breath. Still giggling, a horrified look passes over her face.

"What's wrong?" Mom stands up in a panic.

"I either peed myself. Or my water broke."

TWENTY-ONE

SAGE

ARCHIE AND DAD run into the room, knocking into each other and tipping my salad onto the floor.

"What do we do?" Archie asks, panic rising in his voice.

"Calm down, dear. You had a practice run at this earlier today." Mom is the picture of calm and confident. "Collect her overnight bag and get the car ready. We're going back to the hospital."

Violet Agnes Fischer comes howling into the world at four-thirty in the morning. Pink, pissed off, and perfect.

According to my mother, she settled as soon as she had a little nosh on my sister's breast. "She was hangry. The same way Rose gets."

Apple.

Tree.

We're home now. Well, at Archie and Rose's house. Dad's snoring away on the sofa. He doesn't take up the entire thing like Lee would.

Lee.

Yes, I let myself think of him as super hot, super sexy Lee now. Lee who gives me orgasms and wants puppies with me.

The past twenty-four hours have been completely sleep deprived and a blur. I haven't thought about him outside of telling Rose and avoiding telling my mother.

I texted Elizabeth on my way to the airport we'd have to delay bringing home the puppies. She responded that Cruella would happily keep them for as long as possible. Of course she would.

With Dad napping in here and Mom in the guest room, I sneak into Violet's gender neutral, chic nursery. A twin bed anchors one wall. I guess it's for the night nurse or whoever is on overnight baby duty. Careful of the decorative pillows, I pull back the comforter and crawl under the sheets.

Before giving in to my exhaustion, I check my phone. I'm surprised to see Lee's name when I tap the screen.

I didn't get to say good-bye. Has the baby arrived yet?

Violet Agnes and her mother are doing well.

And her beautiful aunt?

Super sleepy.

Am I picking up our puppies tomorrow?

Oh crap. I forgot to text him.

Cruella is keeping them until I get back.

We still want to get them together?

My question is more than a confirmation of picking up the puppies. We haven't really talk-talked since being naked. I'm all about Namaste and going with the flow, but his words from the Fourth gnaw around the edges of my confidence.

Of course. Nothing's changed.

This isn't a conversation I want to have via text speak. Contemplating his words, I roll my lips together while I try to think of a response.

Are we sure they're safe with her and her band of miscreants?

Elizabeth will make sure they're fine.

Excellent.

Before I can respond, another text arrives.

I miss you.

My finger hovers over my screen. I want to ask as a friend or more. Instead, I go for simple.

Miss you too. Going to nap. xo

The xo might be too much. I'm confused by the current status of our friend-relationship. *Frielationship? Friendlations?*

The boundaries have blurred to the point of no longer existing.

Distance and a nap are probably the smartest solutions right now.

When I wake up it's nearly dark outside. I find Dad in the kitchen warming up pizza in the microwave.

"You want some?" He points to the box still sitting on the counter.

I nod and yawn. "What time is it?"

"After eight. I didn't want to wake you. Your mom went back to the hospital to bring dinner to the kids." He hands me a hot plate with a wedge of pizza.

"Thank you."

He takes a seat next to me at the counter. "How are you

doing, Aunt Sage?"

"Wow. I'm an aunt." I pause with my fork near my mouth. "Congrats on being a grandfather."

He smiles, looking both proud and tired. Suddenly he seems older to me. He's not only my dad anymore. He's someone's grandfather.

"Are those more gray hairs?" I lean closer to his side.

"Probably. I swear last year I was chasing you and Rose around a playground. It all goes by in a blink. Everyone says that, but sometimes clichés are truth."

I want to hug him so I do. "You're young. Rose is a young mom. No one in this family is getting old. I won't allow it."

He returns my hug with a squeeze. "My sweet girl."

"I feel like you're going to apologize for forgetting my birthday because Rose is marrying a bohunk."

I can see I've confused him.

"It's a John Hughes movie reference. *Sixteen Candles*?"

His blank stare tells me this is out of his dad wheelhouse. "I don't know what a bohunk is, but I'm certain Archie is not one."

I lean into his side and laugh. "No, Archie Fischer is the exact opposite."

"Good. I like him and he's the father of my grandchild." Dad twists on his stool to face me. "Now what about you?"

"Time to marry off the younger daughter? Have you hired a matchmaker?"

He hums a few notes of "If I Were a Rich Man," making me laugh.

"If?"

"The sentiment is the same. You seem happy in Colorado, even though it's too far away from your family."

"It's a short flight to Phoenix." I bump his shoulder.

"I miss the years when we all lived under one roof. It went

by too fast." He pats my arm. "You didn't answer my question. Are you dating the South African man?"

"It's complicated."

"Is he married?" Dad's eyes hold concern and worry.

"No, of course not. I'd never do that."

"We raised our girls right." He pinches my elbow, a gesture he's done since we were little.

How much of my romantic life, or lack thereof, do I want to share with my father?

"Is he a rapscallion type who seduces heiresses and young ladies for their trust funds?"

The pap photos of Lee and the hotel heiress flash in my mind. "No, I suspect he has his own trust fund."

"Does he know about yours?"

"I never tell people I'm the Blum in Bloom and Board."

"Smart."

"It's easier out there. Almost everyone is from somewhere else. We all have our histories and secrets." Mine being a multi-million dollar trust fund I can't bear to deal with or spend.

"The money is yours to use however you like. It's there whether you acknowledge it or don't. It'll wait for you."

"I know. Someday I'll get used to the idea."

"You could use it for charity work. I wouldn't advise giving it all away, but you could spend some of it on good deeds."

"I thought that's what the family charitable trust does." Being able to write a large check to Elizabeth to cover operating expenses would be amazing and a good way to spend some of my money.

"Of course you can suggest donations for the group, but your trust is to do with what you want. It's your money. No need to feel guilty about having it."

"I do. I didn't earn it. I didn't choose my parents."

He gives me a tight one-arm hug. "Some kids would feel entitled by a trust fund. You have never acted like a spoiled child."

"Except living in a condo in Aspen rent free and wasting my life being an exercise instructor."

"Your mother and I think of you as a lovable squatter. I know you believe I don't approve of your career choice, but it's only because I don't ever want you to settle. Or not think you're good enough to follow your dreams. Do I wish those dreams included working for your grandfather's company? Of course. But you're going to make your own path."

"I was miserable working in product development after college. I only did it for a year to make you and Mom happy."

"We know. You being miserable makes no one happy. You're happy in Aspen."

He tugs on my earlobe, another gesture from my childhood. It was our secret code for I love you when I became too cool to give my dad a hug in public. I'm not too cool now. I turn and hug him with all that I have.

"I love you, Daddy." I haven't called him Daddy in years.

He pauses before squeezing me back. "Love you."

We pull apart and sit quietly for a few moments.

"Will we meet this Zulu warrior someday?"

I giggle at the image of Lee in a loincloth holding a spear. "I hope so."

We're in an odd place, Lee and me. I'm still processing his comments on the Fourth and his casual texts since. I feel like he changed the game, but hasn't told me what the new rules are. Or even if we're on the same team.

TWENTY-TWO

STAN

MY FLIGHT LANDS in Chicago and I impatiently stand in the taxi queue. The sweltering humidity of July dampens my shirt in the short time I wait.

Miserably cold in the winter, stifling in the summer, this city reminds me of various levels of hell. Perhaps it's because I'm here to meet with the devil himself—my father.

I've been summoned. Forty-eight hours ago I received my itinerary in an email from his secretary.

Zero discussion. Zero chance to refuse or have any say at all.

Plane tickets purchased and a hotel room reserved.

We have a meeting scheduled for nine tomorrow morning. In his office.

The warm feeling of family is almost too much to absorb.

I'm hot, tired, and cranky by the time I check into my hotel. My father has more than enough room in his vast apartment, but I'd rather have some distance between us. This way I have a place to escape to and lick my wounds if necessary.

Once in my room, I order something to eat and start the shower. I shed my airplane and cab infiltrated clothes, leaving a pile of them on the bathroom floor. Stepping into the warm spray, my mind goes back to Sage in my bathroom holding plastic bin bags.

A few months and a lifetime ago our friendship was easy and simple.

I don't want to go back to being "just friends" and certainly not stay "friends with benefits" like she thinks we're at now. Or whatever nonsense I spouted on the Fourth. I felt backed into a corner and I certainly wasn't going to confess my feelings to Sage with Tess standing there. Or in front of an audience of hundreds during a fireworks display. My brilliant plan to end our fake relationship so a real one can begin didn't go over so well. It was a disaster.

As the water pours over me, I stop focusing on the mess we are now. There's something real between us. If I haven't fucked everything up and she'll let me untangle the web, this could be more.

Images of naked Sage flow behind my eyelids as I soap my body. My own personal highlight reel of her naked and loving me plays as I drift my hands lower. The soap helps my hand glide over my hard length. My other fingers cup my balls, applying a gentle pressure that will speed up my release. Resting my head on the tiles of the shower, I let my thoughts drift to Sage above me, Sage on my bed naked and trusting me.

I jerk my hips and increase my rhythm before falling over the edge.

I brace my hand on the wall, steadying myself while I catch my breath. My heartbeats slow and regulate themselves. If only my emotions could return to normal.

I brush the lapel of my charcoal suit, waiting for the elevator to ascend to my father's office. My white shirt is starched, but I skipped the tie.

A stern woman around my age greets me when I step off the elevator. According to the large gold lettering on the far wall of the lobby, my father's company fills the entire floor.

"You must be Stanley." She extends her hand. "I'm Virginia, your father's executive director."

"Lee." Her hand is cold and limp when I shake it. Dressed all in black with a touch of white at her collar, she reminds me of a solemn priest. "My father is Stanley. I'm Lee."

"Oh, he didn't tell me. I'll make a note in your file."

Of course I have a file in his office. Most likely it includes only the essentials: birthdate, current address, recent gifts so as not to repeat. What else would anyone here need to know about me?

"How's the rugby season going so far?" She makes idle small talk as we walk down a long hall flanked by glass enclosed offices on one side and a sea of cubicles on the other.

Clearly my file needs to be updated. "I missed most of the first half due to a broken ankle. My coach has me on limited play. So to answer your question, it *vokken* sucked."

She flinches slightly. "Did your father know?"

"Wasn't it updated in my file?" My voice is ice.

With a quick shake of her head, she frowns. "I'll make a note to follow the club's website."

We've reached a set of dark wood double-doors with a neat desk sitting to the left. I assume the desk is hers with its tidy stacks of papers and a framed picture of her in a wedding dress with her groom.

She raps her knuckles on the door twice and both open automatically. "Mr. Barnard, your son has arrived."

My father's desk sits another twenty feet away, surrounded

by glass windows looking down on Chicago. He glances up and nods, but doesn't speak.

"Can I get you anything to drink? Coffee? Tea? Water?"

"Water, please." My throat feels dry and my hands dampen with nervous sweat. These reactions only annoy me. First rule with the devil: don't show weakness. I clear my throat. "Flat, no ice."

Virginia quietly leaves the room and the doors click closed behind me.

"Fancy trick you have with the remote." I'm still standing near the back wall.

"Are you going to lurk around in the shadows back there or sit in a chair like an adult?" He focuses on me.

It's going to be one of those visits. I haven't had a chewing out by him since the pap photos with the heiress. It's typically enough for him to chastise me via email or curt phone call. I've done something offensive to require him to meet with me in person.

I wrack my brain trying to think what it could be.

"How's the ankle?"

Ah, so news of my injury did travel to Chicago. I take a seat at his enormous desk. My chair is lower than his, putting me at a disadvantage and making me feel like a small boy.

"How did you hear about it?"

"Your mother rang me." Annoyance is evident in his voice. "You should have let me know."

"I didn't want to bother you. A minor hairline fracture and it's healed now. Good as new."

His eyes are the same color as mine, but colder. I stare into them, trying to see more than a shared genetic trait.

Virginia returns with my glass of water on a tray and quickly leaves after handing it to me. If she feels the tension in the room, she's an expert at ignoring it.

"It might be time to give up the rugby dream and grow up." He taps an expensive looking pen on his fancy leather desk blotter. "You're far too old to play professionally at this point. And if you're encountering injuries and setbacks in your hobby club, you're a fool to keep wasting your time."

I twist my mouth and exhale as if his words punched me in the gut. Our staring contest continues. I don't dare look away and concede a victory to him. In my lap, I dig my thumbnail into my palm to avoid cursing at him.

"Nothing to say, Stanley?"

"It's Lee."

"No, your name is Stanley. You're too old for childish nicknames. I need to see some effort on your part in the coming years."

In three years I'll be thirty. "Are you threatening my trust?"

"I can't do that, but I expect you to demonstrate your ability to be an adult sooner rather than later."

I shift my focus to the skyline behind him while toying with the band of my watch. "I work. I have a life in Aspen."

"You make cocktails in a hotel bar. You get your picture taken. Those are not careers. When you finished university and wanted to play rugby, I supported the idea thinking you'd have the drive and commitment to go pro. Apparently, I was wrong."

"I'm a top competitor in our league. Team captain. Respected."

"It's an amateur club in a ski town. No one takes it seriously. You had a professional career laid out for you and you threw it away."

I take it seriously, but I don't bother saying this out loud. "I played and got injured. Game over. It happens all the time. You probably don't care to hear that my contract with the ski company has been renewed for another year."

He scowls at me. "Living life on your looks isn't something to brag about. It's embarrassing to hear my female employees twittering about my son in his underwear on some website. Beyond embarrassing, it's disrespectful to me. And your mother."

"I've never posed in my skivvies." I sit forward in my chair, pushing myself higher to be on the same level as him. "Mum is proud of everything I do."

"Swim trunks. Underwear. Same thing. Your mother is a simple woman who lives on the other side of the world and doesn't have to face repercussions from her son's actions splashed all over tabloid media outlets."

"I doubt anything I do affects you. Or your business. That's what matters, isn't it? The money in the banks?"

"That money is what allows you to live your silly life in Aspen."

"It's not silly."

"Do you plan to be doing the same thing in two years? Five years? You're going to wake up one day and realize you're an old guy trying to live in a young man's world. You'll have nothing to show for your life."

Something clicks. "You're jealous."

"Of what? You?" He shoves back from his desk. Standing over me, he's in full intimidation mode. "I made my first million by thirty. I turned it into ten by thirty-five. You think you're on track to beat that?"

"It's not a competition, Father."

"Like hell it's not. Life isn't about the journey. It's winners and losers. Those who succeed and those who fail."

"Funny you didn't mention when you married my mother or when I was born in your timeline of major life events."

"I wasn't talking about the emotional baggage which comes

along with living life to its fullest potential."

His words should hurt. I don't even flinch. My face gives nothing away.

Emotions are weakness.

Relationships are baggage.

"Let's cut to why I was summoned here. Is there something you need me to sign?" I lean forward.

"Didn't Virginia send you the invite? I expect you to attend a fundraiser we're sponsoring. There's a day of golfing, which you can skip, but you are expected at the dinner. It's not optional. All the partners will have their families there."

Ah. "Keeping up appearances?"

"It's an important event for the firm. Given you benefit from our success, the very least you can do is show up and look good. Apparently, the one thing you're excellent at doing."

If I had a dollar for every dig . . . I kind of do. A reminder of this fact weighs heavy on my wrist. I love this watch, but it's a symbol of being my father's pawn.

"Have Virginia text me with the details. I'll be there."

"It's a little late to bring a date, so try to behave yourself with the wives and daughters." He fires a parting shot.

I twist the watchband around my wrist. "I learned from the best to always separate business from pleasure, Father."

"I'm pleased something stuck." His phone beeps.

Virginia's voice tells him it's time for his next meeting. It could be an excuse to cut things short with me.

I'm beyond caring at this point.

"I'll see you tomorrow evening. If there is anything else, let me know before then. My flight is first thing in the morning on Friday."

Already scribbling something on a stack of papers, he doesn't notice when I stand. "That's fine. Fine."

The door magically opens for me when I approach. I turn to say good-bye and find him facing the window.

Dismissed.

I thumb open another button on my shirt the second the elevator doors close.

My watch shows the time as half past nine. I flew a thousand miles for thirty minutes of face time with my father. Now I'm stuck in this city for another two days.

Not a waste of my time at all.

I clearly have nothing better to do with my time.

My instinct is to find a dark bar and drink whisky.

The muggy air on the street permeates my dress shirt within minutes as I stride through the stragglers of the morning rush hour. I head in the direction of the lake, needing the comfort of nature.

It's not the sea, but there's a breeze of fresh air when I reach Navy Pier. I pass the Ritz and resist the temptation to go upstairs, pack my bags, and fly back to Aspen today.

I won't act the petulant child and prove my father right in his opinions of my life.

I've learned in modeling to play types of personalities, shedding and adapting personas as needed. Surely I can act the dutiful son for one evening.

The longer strands of my hair fall into my face with the breeze. I shove them away, momentarily missing my ability to pull back my hair. Then I remember Sage's eyes when she saw the bun was cut off. Delight and lust mixed together into a new expression of happiness.

She's somewhere in this same city. My fingers coil around my phone in my front pocket. I've resisted phoning her since my arrival last night, but I need a dose of her spirit after thirty minutes with my father.

I send her a text while walking back to my hotel. If she doesn't respond, I'll call her.

Repeatedly if necessary.

I can't stand knowing she's here and I'm not with her.

TWENTY-THREE

SAGE

"IT'S LIKE WITH the puppies. I didn't consider a puppy until Cruella De Vil was going to take all of them, doing who knows what with them in her fenced yard in Basalt. You should've seen the look in her eyes when she talked about how many puppies she could foster. All of them! I wouldn't trust her to not make them into a coat."

"What does this have to do with Lee?" For some bizarre reason, Zoe can't keep up. We've spent the better part of this afternoon day drinking in the shade of an umbrella on a restaurant patio in Wrigleyville. It's been a productive day. I'm so happy she's home in Chicago and our days overlap.

"How much wine did you drink?" I lift the mostly empty bottle from the cooler on the table.

"I'm not drunk. You're not making sense. One minute you were moaning about Lee and now you're rambling about 101 Dalmatians and Basalt. I admit, you lost me."

I pour more white wine into our glasses and drop in a couple of ice cubes. "The answer might be more wine, not less."

"Fine. Start from the beginning again."

"I like dogs. Everyone knows puppies are adorable. Until recently, I didn't think I had a chance to have a puppy of my own."

"Are you talking about real dogs or Lee?"

"The puppies represent Lee."

She rolls her wrist, silently telling me to give her more.

I skim over the smoothie and arrangement before jumping back into the puppy metaphor.

"Lee is my puppy." I sip my icy wine. "Not until Cruella De Vil showed up ready to write a check for Lee, did I realize how much I wanted a puppy."

"Wait, some woman wanted to buy Lee? Like an escort?"

"No! He's not for sale."

"You said . . . oh, never mind." She lifts her glass and swallows a long gulp. "Let me see if I understand the root of the problem. You've finally admitted to yourself you like Lee as more than a friend. Then some other woman comes into the picture proclaiming you can't have him, and you realize how much you want to fight to keep him? Am I close?"

I nod. "See? I knew the Cruella De Vil story would explain it."

"You're crazy."

"Right, right, moving past that. This is the part where you eagerly agree to my madcap scheme to convince him to stop being my friend."

"You don't want to be friends with him anymore?"

"I want to stop pretending to date him. I want to real date him. With real sex and dates."

"I think you've already had the real sex."

"Oh, it was real. Real amazing." I sigh and rest my chin on my hand with my elbow on the table.

She shakes her head. "Off track, Sage. You were talking about plotting to win him over?"

"Have you never watched a romantic comedy movie from the '80s or '90s?"

Her blank stare answers my question.

"That's not really important. You simply need to say you agree with whatever plan I hatch up and are willing to get messy executing it if necessary."

"Why can't you walk next door and have a normal conversation with him? Like adults? In this century? Who are not in a movie?"

"That's not how this works. What if he rejects me?"

"A crazy gesture doesn't guarantee he won't. It will save on time and humiliation. For everyone involved, which doesn't include me."

"You're no help whatso . . . ever." The sun and wine are beginning to be too much.

"I have an idea!" Zoe slams her hand a little too hard on the table, tipping over the saltshaker.

"An extra complicated one involving a small herd of pygmy goats and a lot of balloons?"

Her mouth hangs open as she at squints me. "Are the balloons tied to the goats?"

"That's brilliant! We float the goats with balloons. He comes outside to check out the cuteness and whammy."

She silently pulls my wine glass to the other side of the table. "I'm cutting you off."

I roll my bottom lip out in a pout. "What's your idea?"

"Okay, pay attention. It's very simple."

I lean across the table, holding my breath in anticipation.

"Lee already likes you. Probably has for a while."

"This isn't a plan at all."

"Stay with me. Did you ever stop to think about the whole setup? A fake relationship?"

"Not so fake if the orgasms were real." I try to sneak my glass back and she flicks my hand away.

"Think about it."

"The sex?"

"No, the setup. Why did he need a fake girlfriend? And why would he commit to getting puppies with a fake girlfriend he was going to break up with?"

I narrow my eyes as I try to remember. "He said something about giving him breathing space from the masses of chicks who want to bang him."

"He called them chicks? He refers to sex as banging?" A look of disgust mars her pretty face.

"I might be paraphrasing."

"It doesn't make sense."

"Isn't paraphrasing the right word?" I sip my water. "Maybe we should order some food."

"That's a good idea. You used the right word, but we're going to need food and to be more sober to figure this out."

I pat her arm, sappy tears filling my eyes. "You're the best kind of friend."

"The kind who will day drink with you and listen to your babbling?"

I nod. "You're also really pretty, but not a bitch because you think you're prettier than everyone else. You're beautiful because you don't care about your looks. "

After I stand and give her a hug, she waves over the waiter to order us some food.

Halfway through my grilled chicken Caesar salad, I'm feeling better. The food gives me a full belly, which makes me sleepy.

"I still can't figure out why he'd need to pretend to be in a relationship with you. He already has a reputation for drawing boundaries with women. Lee emits the unattainable vibe pretty strongly." Zoe keeps jabbing her fry into ketchup as she speaks. The poor potato is covered in red. "Was there an event or something he needed a presentable date for?"

I shake my head.

"Wedding? Those are quicksand for single men."

"Do you know anyone who's ever been trapped in quicksand?"

She gives me an odd look. "No, have you?"

"No. Yet we're all afraid of falling into quicksand and dying. Why? It's completely irrational."

"Excellent point, although it's also completely off the subject."

"I made him drink liquefied kale and he asked me to pretend to date him in trade. Then he suggested we get puppies, but I had to come here for Rose. We don't have the puppies yet. And maybe never will. That's the whole event thread."

"It's a pretty short timeline from smoothie to puppies to sex."

"Not that short. Weeks passed. It's been over two months since he broke his ankle."

"Still. No one could see you when you first kissed. It wasn't for show."

My lips tingle in memory of when he kissed me in the kitchen. "Completely out of the blue."

"Or not. I'm going with my gut on this. He likes you."

"You've read too many books and they've addled your brain."

"Okay, Louisa May. Someday I'm going to say I told you so."

I bob my head side to side and smirk at her. "Someday is not today."

My phone buzzes and chirps on the table.

"Maybe that's Lee." She reaches her hand out for it, but I'm too quick.

The screen displays one word: Stan.

"Damn you." I show her the front.

"I told you—"

"You only get to say it once, so you might want to sit on it." I flip her off with a glower.

"Are you going to answer it?"

"He never calls me."

"Then pick up!" I'm not expecting her to grab the phone out of my hand.

"Hello. Sage's phone. Zoe speaking." She grins at me. "She's fine. Right here in fact. Uh huh."

Torn between tackling her for the phone and not wanting to know what he's saying because I'm playing it cool, I lean away from the table and grip the arms of my chair.

"That's interesting. Uh huh."

I screw my lips together and twist them to the side.

"Wrigleyville. We're day drinking at Orso's. You've heard of it?" She laughs like they're old friends. "Of course. It's famous."

Now she's giggling.

"My puppy," I mumble and cross my arms, staring at the foot traffic on the sidewalk. "Mine."

"I think she's getting cranky we're chatting so long. I should let you talk to Sage. Oh? Oh. Okay. Mmm hmm. Okay. Sounds good." She pulls the phone away from her ear, glances at the screen, then hands it back to me.

"Hello? Lee?" I notice the screen is black and tap it, bringing up my home screen. "He hung up?"

She shrugs and sips her wine. "Guess he had to go."

"Were you even talking to him? All that giggling and moaning 'oh, oh, mmm hmm' sounded like a fake conversation."

"I promise you, he was on the phone."

"Then why did you hog all his attention and not let me speak to him if I'm the one he called?" I drain the watery remains in my wineglass.

"I can tell you what he said, if you stop pouting for a minute."

I wave her off. The heart flutters from seeing his name on my phone morph into full out annoyance. I miss him and we're in a strange place between friends and more. "He can tell me himself. I don't need to hear it secondhand from you."

Leaning on her elbow on the table, she rests her chin on her hand. "Don't be cranky. Trust me."

I focus on eating my salad, stabbing the half-soggy croutons and spearing chunks of chicken.

Our waiter appears, and asks if we need more wine. I'm half tempted to say yes, but we've finished one bottle already.

"I'll have an iced tea. Sage?" Zoe asks.

"I'm fine," I mumble. I'm unable to shake the bummed feeling settling over me like an ugly Snuggly. It's comforting and familiar.

When he returns, the waiter's shadow blocks the sun. He looms over the table from the other side of the metal fencing separating us from the pedestrians.

"Do either of you ladies need anything?" His voice sounds deeper and his accent changed. "Coffee, tea? Me?"

"Oh boy," I mutter. "We're going to leave you a good tip. No need to turn on the charm act now."

The sun momentarily blinds me when I glance up to give him a dirty look. I have to shade my eyes with my hand to see him and tilt my head back farther. And farther.

He's not our waiter.

TWENTY-FOUR

STAN

I CAN'T SEE her eyes behind her sunglasses, but Sage isn't smiling or leaping out of her chair with joy to see me.

"Well, if it isn't Satan himself standing in the flesh," she whispers.

I give her my best devilish grin. "I'm not Satan. You mean my father. I can see how you confuse the two of us with the same name and everything."

"Evil is as evil does."

"Sage," Zoe chastises me. "Hi, Lee."

She gives me a little wave and I mirror it back at her. "Hi, Zoe. Lovely day for drinking."

"It was," Sage grumbles and crosses her arms.

Ignoring her sourpuss friend, Zoe smiles at me. "You should join us. Tell us what brings you to Chicago."

"He can tell us from his side of the fence. The patio is for paying customers and their dogs. Apparently." Sage points at a pair of panting brown and white lap dogs lying in the shade beneath the next table.

Ignoring the snark, I walk around the barricade and slip

into the seat next to her.

"That's taken."

I hand her bag to Zoe who tucks it on top of hers on the remaining empty chair.

"I'm here to see my father," I answer Zoe's question.

"Wait a second, your father lives in Chicago? I don't know any Stanley Barnards."

"It's a big city. He's lived here for almost ten years now."

"What does he do in Chicago?"

"Makes money. That's his sole focus in life. Making more money and reveling in the power that comes from having a humongous bank account and a top floor suite of offices."

Sage blinks at me. "You never told me."

"I don't like discussing him."

Her expression softens and she frowns. "I haven't been a good friend to you."

"Why?" I pull free a strand of hair twisted in her sunglasses.

"I thought we were doing the whole don't ask, don't tell thing about our personal stuff. You know all about my crazy family."

"You found out my favorite dessert my mother baked for me and copied it. Still one of the nicest things anyone has ever done for me."

"Aww," Zoe whispers from the other side of the table.

"Right?"

"What are you doing here?" Sage asks.

"I'm visiting my father." I squint at her in confusion. "I told you that less than two minutes ago. How much wine have you had?"

"No, I mean here at this restaurant. Right now? Don't suppose you happened to be randomly strolling around Wrigleyville on a Wednesday afternoon." She points at Zoe. "That would be too much of a coincidence."

"I told him where to find us. He asked a question. I gave him an answer." The two of them have a silent staring contest behind their sunglasses.

"I wanted to see you. Your texts have been short and vague. I feel like it's been a month since we've talked."

"It's only been ten days."

"That's too long. It's good to see you." I extend my arm along the back of her chair.

Zoe announces she needs the ladies' room and leaves us.

"How are you? How are Rose and the baby?"

A small smile fights to break free from her pout. "They're good. Violet is perfect. I'm basically doing nothing but getting in the way. My mother is a tornado of grandmotherly action. Dad and I spend most of our time hanging out on the couch, out of the chaos."

"Do you have a picture?" It's an excuse to lean closer to her. I'm not one for admiring babies. They all look the same to me.

Sage shows me a picture of her niece gripping the pale blue strands of her hair. "Isn't she beautiful?"

"I see she's a fan of the new color. I think this one's my favorite." I let the silky hair slide through my fingers.

"Stan." She leans away. "What are you doing here?"

"I miss you. You left Aspen in a rush and we still need to talk."

"Talk."

"Not here. Not with Zoe listening."

"She's in the bathroom."

"I don't want to be interrupted."

"I'm very busy with the baby."

"You said not ten minutes ago you're sitting around and getting in the way. Give me an hour. Or better, have dinner with me. Take me to your favorite restaurant in the city."

She gives me a side-eye full of doubt. "If your father has lived here for ten years, certainly you've visited all the major sites before."

"It's not my favorite city. I typically order room service at the Ritz or a pizza from Malnati's. I'm never here long enough to explore the city."

"That's . . . a travesty. We're a Giordino's family."

"Is this a deal breaker? The stuff of the Capulets and Montagues?"

"We take our pies seriously here. Shakespearean tragedies could be written about this city and our pizza."

"I've never had Giordino's."

Her gasp is nearly silent, but her mouth hangs open in shock. "You're missing out."

"Then show me. Make me fall in love with your city."

Zoe must be hiding out inside the restaurant. I'll have to tell her thank you later.

"A few hours together. For years we've hung out together. Let's do that."

She studies me. A few minutes stretch into forever as I wait for her to accept my proposal or turn me down.

"Okay, with one caveat."

I exhale in relief. "Okay?"

She clears her throat and sips some water, then straightens up the table.

Fighting the tug of a smile, I observe her nervous stalling. "The parameters?"

Her attention settles somewhere over my shoulder. "No discussions of past or future. No expectations. Let's be two friends hanging out, enjoying the city. Deal?"

"I can't promise I won't fall in love . . . with the city, but I'll do my best." All this talk makes me think she's setting boundaries again. I don't know why, but I'm going to find out.

Silence settles between us until Zoe returns. "Is it safe?"

"I'm going to show Lee around the city. He's never had Giordino's."

"What? Is this your first visit?" Her mouth hangs open, mirroring Sage's.

"I know! See?" Sage hits my shoulder with the back of her hand.

"I'm trying to remedy the errors of my ways." My words hold more meaning than eating pizza. I hope Sage understands I could give two rats' asses about being a tourist here. I want to spend time with her and clear the air. If sweating through the streets of the city is what it's going to take, I'm up for anything if we can finally talk face to face.

"Want to join us?" she asks Zoe.

Zoe looks at me for advice. I shake my head no. "I'm going to pass. In this heat? I'm crispy from drinking in the sun. Give me air conditioning and a nap."

Her yawn is as fake as my enthusiasm for sightseeing.

We say our good-byes and pour ourselves into a cab. At least it has AC. "Where to first?"

"Art Institute," she tells the cabbie.

I trail behind her through the Art Institute as she points out the highlights of the collection. We replicate the poses of American Gothic and Sunday Afternoon at the Grand Jette. I snap selfies of us with our stoic expressions before we crack up in fits of giggles. The security guard shushes us.

My cheeks hurt from smiling when we spill out the main doors into the late afternoon warmth. The heat and humidity no longer bother me.

Sage clasps my hand and drags me down the steps. "We have to go to the Bean next."

I entwine our fingers and pull ahead of her, heading north to Millennium Park. She jogs to keep up, our joined hands swinging between us. The silver reflection of Cloud Gate, aka the Bean, shimmers in between the green leaves of the trees in the park.

Other tourists crowd around the sculpture, playing with their distorted reflections in its shiny surface. Our silliness continues from the Institute as we pose and take our own selfies.

Sage tosses her head back, laughing at her own reflection. I snap a picture and immediately make it her profile image on my phone. She looks joyous.

There's only so many selfies and silly faces a man can make before he's had enough. I reach that point after five.

I may model, but I'm not vain. There's nothing more boring than standing around having my picture taken. Unless it's sitting and listening to my father speak.

Which reminds me . . .

"Do you have plans for tomorrow night?" I ask.

She hesitates before responding. I don't know if she's mentally checking her calendar or inventing an excuse in her mind. "I think I have something planned with my parents. I have to go as Archie's date because there is no way Rose is leaving the house to squeeze herself into a cocktail dress."

My frown is automatic.

"I'm sorry. Did you have something planned already? I can try to get out of it, but it's a company thing and we're the happy smiling people face of Bloom and Board."

"It's okay. Some fancy party with my father's firm."

"I'm sure you fill out a suit nicely." Her eyes become unfocused as if she's imagining me in a suit right now.

Memories of our last conversation at the Aspen Music tent hit me in the gut. "Speaking of fancy parties, I want to apologize for what I said on the Fourth."

"Why do you think you did something requiring an apology?" Her tone is dry and on the far side of sarcastic.

"I'm sorry."

"For what?"

"Is this a test?"

"You should know what you're apologizing for."

Where do I begin?

Her phone rings. She holds up a finger before answering it. "Hold that apology."

I watch her reflection get smaller as she walks away from me. Eventually she disappears from the reflection. I spin around to find her, not wanting to lose sight of her. Finally I spot her blond hair near the shade of a row of trees.

For all I know she's chatting up an old boyfriend who still loves her. Unlike my connection to this city, she has roots here. An expanding family and old friends like Zoe who all adore her. I tilt my head back to see the skyscrapers of downtown. In one of those hundreds of offices is a man who shares my name. He feels as impersonal and distant as ever despite his proximity.

Sage paces, still talking. I take out my own phone and check messages. I'm missing some training sessions this week and Drew reminds me to take advantage of the hotel gym. He even attaches a list of workouts, as if I don't have our schedule memorized. He asks about my ankle and I assure him it's fine other than some swelling on the plane.

I'm tapping away when she returns.

"Sorry for that."

"What are you apologizing for?" I echo her words from earlier.

"Ha ha. Well played, Holmes." Her voice sounds light, but

a new tension tightens her shoulders.

"Everything okay?"

"Oh, yeah. That was my dad. He wants me to meet with some lawyers tomorrow morning."

"A ha! You are on the lam, hiding out in Aspen." I give her a cheeky grin.

"I wish." She doesn't elaborate.

"Do you want to walk up to Navy Pier? It's only about thirty minutes from here."

"I love the pier, but I should probably head home."

"Please stay. At least walk with me. We're both going north. You can jump into a cab at any time. Or I'll call a car for you." Having access to my father's accounts here can do something good for once.

"Okay, let's walk."

We stroll up Michigan Avenue. Our arms touch, brushing against each other, but we don't hold hands again. As we walk, she points out various sites and trivia about the city. It's clear to me how much she loves her hometown.

"Have you ever had a Chicago dog?"

"No, but I'm starving. Lead the way."

She steers us a couple blocks west to a place she swears is a Chicago institution and a must on any tour.

"Shouldn't you be a vegan or lactose-pescatarian?" I ask while we stand in line for steamed meat.

"Why? Because I'm a former dancer? Or I teach barre? I love me some meat." She licks and then smacks her lips.

"You're utterly ridiculous, *gogga*."

"So are you if you think I'm going to pass up hot dogs and brats. Or cheese."

"I think I assumed you were a hippie vegan when we first met."

"Really?" The thought makes her laugh. "I thought you were a playboy player."

Her laughter stops.

"I guess first impressions can be wrong."

"Sometimes they are."

"Do you still think of me as a playboy player?"

"No, you're a homebody with a pretty face. All those books in your office dispelled the illusion you have a sex dungeon."

My brain can't keep up with her words. "Sex dungeon? My office?"

She flutters her hand in front of her. "Nothing."

"When were you in my sex dungeon?"

The family of four in matching Disney T-shirts takes a collective step away from us. The father gives me a dirty look while the mother sizes me up and winks. She must read the same books as my mother.

"You don't have one. The women of Aspen will be devastated."

"You snooped in my condo."

Color pinks her cheeks and neck.

"Busted."

"I checked to see it wasn't a trophy room dedicated to your enormous, yet delicate male ego."

"You sound disappointed it wasn't."

"I was surprised by all of your books. I feel guilty for being surprised. I didn't doubt you could read. That's not it. I'm surprised you find time to read among all of your oth-er . . . activities."

Slowly, we move forward in the line. I let Sage order for both of us, telling her to get me whatever she's having.

We step to the side and wait for the guys behind the counter to assemble our hot dogs. "You should know by now most of the rumors about my life are for show. Or distraction."

"I do. Now."

Her number is called and she collects the two paper trays of loaded dogs. "Ready for the best thing you'll have in your mouth any time soon?"

I know her words are meant to be funny, but they're not what I want to hear. "We'll see about that."

"Challenge accepted."

We squeeze onto two stools at a long counter. Somewhere under a mound of peppers, pickles, onions, tomatoes and mustard sits a frankfurter. I think. Hoisting the bun to my mouth, I open wide. I bite and chew, being carefully watched by Sage the entire time.

I nod, my mouth too full to speak.

She takes a bite of hers and mustard squeezes out the side, landing on her cheek.

"Good?" she asks after swallowing.

"Amazing. You have a little something on your cheek."

Her tongue peeks out and licks the corners of her mouth. She's not even close to getting it. I could use my napkin and wipe it away for her. But where's the fun in that?

"Hold still." She freezes as I lean in close. I swipe my tongue along her skin, removing the mustard.

Her breath hitches in her throat and her pupils dilate. I'm still invading her personal space, waiting for a sign. Or her to grab my neck, pull me down into a kiss in the middle of this dive.

A guy can hope.

"Thanks," she whispers.

"You're welcome." I lean back and take another bite of the hot dog. It's good, but I crave something else to wrap my lips around.

TWENTY-FIVE

SAGE

AFTER OUR HOT dog feast, we meander our way back to Lee's hotel. He's staying at the Ritz.

"This was my grandmother's favorite hotel. We'd come here for fancy lunches and she'd order me chicken tenders. They're still my favorite."

I'm babbling about breaded chicken. I need something to distract me from the feeling of Lee licking mustard off my cheek. Had we not been in the middle of a crowded hot dog joint, I might have straddled him. Or if he hadn't stopped when he did. I was five seconds from losing my mind.

My buzz from the earlier wine is long gone. Dad's call about meeting with the trust attorney's in the morning sobered me right up. The hot dog helped absorb any remaining wine.

"Want to come upstairs?" Lee asks. "Or hang out in the lobby? We don't have to go to my room. I'm not asking you to come up there and have sex with me. We can talk."

Nervous Lee is new to me. I kind of like him.

"I have to go, but let's text before you fly home. I might end up on baby duty."

"When are you flying back to Aspen?"

"My original return date isn't until the end of the month, but I don't think I can last much longer. I need sleep. I need privacy. I really need to get away from my family." I love them all dearly, but too much together time can ruin a perfectly good relationship between grown children and parents.

Bless them.

"I'll pick you up when you come back."

"I can call Darren."

He holds his hand over his heart. "You prefer Darren over me? I'm wounded. I owe you almost two months' worth of rides."

"It's true. You do owe me." I give him a flirty wink because I'm the Queen of Mixed Signals today. I blame the day drinking.

Great idea while it's happening, but it never ends well later in the day.

"We clean up well." I straighten Dad's bowtie on his tuxedo and brush his lapel.

"Thanks for being my date tonight. Your mother doesn't want to leave Rose alone with the baby so soon."

I square my shoulders and adjust the sash at my waist. Rose's dress is a beautiful shade of deep pink, almost fuchsia. We don't have the same body type or coloring, but it looks okay on me. I'm not trying to impress anyone at the fundraiser tonight.

Mom claps her hands when she sees me. "Oh, you look like you're going to prom."

I catch Rose's eyes. "Is that a good thing?"

"The dress looks gorgeous on you. I'll probably never fit into it again, so wear it in good health and enjoy."

"Ready?" Archie asks, holding his car keys on one finger.

"You're a good sport for still coming tonight. We promise we won't have him out late." Dad kisses Rose on the top of her head and then gives Mom a little peck on the lips.

She whispers something to him and his cheeks flush with color. He stands straighter as he gives her a wink. "You have a deal."

I don't even want to know.

As we walk into the ballroom at the Ritz, I realize I don't know anything about this fundraiser. A seat at a table needed to be filled and I, the dutiful daughter, agreed.

I wistfully hope they'll have a passed tray of chicken tenders, but I doubt they'll be fancy enough for this shindig. Lee is somewhere upstairs. Maybe I can sneak out and see him. Would ditching my dad for Lee make me a terrible daughter? He has Archie to keep him company. The two of them are like long lost frat brothers with all their inside jokes and back slapping hugs.

The check-in table displays a sign for the brain tumor charity along with the logos of corporate sponsors. Among them I see my family's company, Bloom and Board. At the top, in the largest font is SB Partners, Ltd.

"SB Partners must have donated big bucks to be the top sponsor," I whisper to my father as we enter the room.

"Apparently brain tumor research is a trendy cancer right now." Dad frowns and tugs at his bowtie. "No disease should be considered 'cool' or trendy. I don't understand people."

I still his hand and readjust the tie. "As long as it brings money and attention, then it's a good thing, right?"

My father's sister died from a brain tumor ten years ago. Ever since, Mom and Dad have heavily donated to support research for a cure. They copied her favorite chair and ten percent from every sale goes into the family charitable fund. The Rachel is one of their bestsellers.

Gray and metallic silver decorate the room and tables. Like most fundraising galas, the vibe is festive, but somber.

Archie offers to get us drinks and weaves his wave over to the bar. Dad and I scan the silent auction items.

I stop short when I see a condo in Aspen as one of the lots. "Look, it's in the same complex as ours. Are you donating my condo?"

Dad reads the description before answering. "Unless your mother did this without telling me, I'm unaware of it. We've offered the company's box seats at a Cubs game."

"Mom probably added it last minute and forgot to mention to me strangers will be spending," I pause to read the description, "a glamorous week in a luxurious condo located in the heart of Aspen during the upcoming ski season."

"Sounds like a nice place. Maybe I should bid." Dad picks up the pen. I know he's joking, but it's not a bad idea.

"I'll bid for it. The money's going to a good cause. If I win, I won't have to clear out for a week." I write down a bid of a thousand dollars above the opening amount and add my paddle number from my name tag.

"Is it illegal to bid on your own lot?" he asks.

"Not for charity. It's all going to a good cause." We stroll past the rest of the items for auction. Archie returns with alcoholic reinforcement in the form of wine for me and scotch for Dad, who gets pulled into a conversation with a circle of silver haired men.

A rose gold bangle catches my attention and I encourage Archie to bid on it by trying it on.

"It's *rose* gold. It's perfect for a push present. Unless you already bought one?" I ask, thinking maybe I missed it.

"Push present?" He sounds confused.

"Oh no." I hang my head. "You should get her a gift for pushing out a baby for you."

Panic flashes across Archie's face right before he bids the full value of the bracelet. "I didn't know."

"Good thing you have me." I link my arm with his. Archie looks handsome in a navy-gray suit and crisp white shirt.

"I don't know what I'd do without you." He squeezes my hand on his arm and guides us through the crowd to find our table.

Away from the throngs of people, I feel someone staring at me. A familiar tingle travels down my spine. I stop and scan the room.

"Everything all right?" Archie asks.

I nod silently when I spot a familiar pair of eyes focused on me from the silent auction area. In his perfectly cut tuxedo, Lee's the most handsome I've ever seen him.

He quirks a single dark brow, letting his eyes drop to my arm linked with Archie's. There's an unfamiliar heat to his stare.

Could Lee be jealous?

Of Ginger Archie?

My brother-in-law?

Lee weaves through the crowd, keeping his eyes locked on me. A small smile, or maybe it's a snarl, tugs at his lips.

When he's finally close, he towers over both us. He stands in front of me, silent and dangerous.

Archie breaks the silence first and extends his hand. "Hello, I'm Archie Fischer. This is my sister-in-law, Sage Blum."

Lee shakes Archie's hand, his face transforming with a genuine smile that creases the outer corners of his eyes. He faces me. "Nice to meet you. I'm Lee Barnard."

"Nice to meet you, Lee." I place my hand in his. He kisses

the back of it, lingering there with his lips pressed to my skin.

Archie's eyes are wider than dinner plates. "Do you two know each other?"

Dad steps beside me. "Sage, will you introduce me to your boyfriend?"

Boyfriend? I gape at my father, widening my eyes in surprise. As I stare at him, he drops his gaze to my waist where my hand remains in Lee's.

"How? How did you know?" I ask despite standing here holding hands with the South African in question.

"It's written all over both of your faces, sweetheart." Dad smiles warmly at us. "I'm Daniel Blum, Sage's father."

Lee stands straighter. "Nice to meet you, sir."

"Aren't you Stanley Bernard's son?" Archie asks. "The rugby player?"

Lee nods, his smile disappearing. "I prefer to be known as the latter, but the former is also true."

His speech sounds formal and stiff. Not his usual charming self. I study him in his suit. His shoulders are pushed back and tense. A small muscle in his cheek right above his jaw twitches. He balls his hands into fists by his side. He stares at someone behind me.

"Stanley, please introduce me."

I turn to see Lee's same eyes set into an older face. There's no doubt this elegant, overly groomed and tanned man is the senior Stanley. I'd know it even if he hadn't just called Lee by his full name.

"Of course." Lee makes the introductions.

Stanley's eyes light up when he hears my father's name. "Our paths have never crossed before, but I'm very familiar with your company."

"As I am with yours." Dad gives him a stiff smile.

"Wonderful. Maybe we can set up a meeting to discuss taking Bloom and Board public."

I exhale and purse my lips. Not only has Stanley brought up business at a charity gala, he's picked my father's least favorite topic. No matter how large the company gets, my grandfather stipulated it will always remain a family business.

Tensing, I wait for my father's response.

He laughs and pats Stanley on the arm. "I'll save both our time and energies by declining that meeting now. If you'll excuse me, I see someone I need to say hello to."

Dad doesn't elaborate. He doesn't need to. He moves through the room, shaking hands and greeting people.

Lee observes the exchange and I watch him. Our eyes meet. He nods in my father's direction, an amused expression in his eyes. "I like your father."

I smile at him. "I think he likes you, too."

Resolve crosses his features and he presses his lips together. He casually flips open the clasp of his watch and holds it out for his father.

Stanley stares at it like a used tissue. "Why are you giving me your watch?"

"Don't you remember?"

"An old Rolex? No, my apologies, I don't."

"You gave it to me for my eighteenth birthday. I asked for something ridiculously expensive to test you. You didn't even blink."

"Then you should keep it." He tries to hand it back to Lee.

"I don't want it anymore. It was never about the watch."

His father stuffs the watch into the inside pocket of his suit. "Instead of this game of cat and mouse, please cut to the deep meaning behind a watch given by a father to his son. Please enlighten me."

Lee practically bristles with pent up emotions. I gently rest my hand between his shoulder blades to remind him I'm here and on his team. Always.

"I wanted your attention," Lee says with a sigh.

"You have it now." A fake smile pulls at Stanley's mouth. If anyone were to observe him right now and not overhear this conversation, they'd think he is a loving father.

However, I'm not sure he even has a heart.

"It's too late. I wanted you to love me as I was."

His father blinks at him. Confusion clouds his face over Lee's wild request for unconditional love. "Of course I love you. You're my flesh and blood."

"You never tell me. Never."

"I push you to be better, because I love you."

"Maybe you should say the words, Mr. Barnard. Out loud. To your son."

His expression tells me he's not used to being told what to do by a woman, let alone one who has blue hair.

"Try it. Three words. One, two, three." I'm not letting this drop. "I can hold your hand if you need the support."

"She's a cheeky *meisie*, isn't she?" Stanley asks his son.

Lee only smiles and nods, wrapping his arm around my shoulders. "Stubborn too. I suggest you give in. As a member of the Blum Family Trust, you don't want her to hold a grudge."

Poor Lee. He's reverting to the only language his father speaks fluently: money.

"Why, yes, of course. The Blums are a pillar of Chicago's history."

"You make us sound like gangsters hanging out with Capone." The very last thing I want is for Stanley to see dollar signs and steps on the social ladder when he looks at me.

There's a reason I don't blab about my family. Money

changes how people interact with and react to me. Never, not once, has Lee ever looked at me the way his father is now. I wish he were checking out my cleavage or ass rather than seeing me as the golden calf.

Ah, there's a Bible reference I usually get right.

"Sage is my girlfriend."

My mouth opens and I clamp it closed again. Aware two sets of blue eyes are observing me, I attempt to remain stoic.

Girlfriend!

Girlfriend.

Wait, real girlfriend or fake relationship girlfriend?

What game is he playing at? Am I now a pawn in this power struggle with his father?

"I can't deny I'm surprised. You didn't mention a girlfriend at our meeting two days ago. What a smart match you make. Perhaps you can help convince your father going public is the right move."

Stanley's like a raccoon in a trash can. He can't seem to stop digging himself deeper and making a big mess trying to get to his perceived prize.

"And that is precisely why I didn't tell you about Sage." Lee wraps his arm around my waist and whispers in my ear, "I think I'm done here."

I nod in agreement. "Me, too."

Dad stands a few feet away, carefully observing the conversation. I recognize his posture from dance recitals when I was little. He's there with his full support, but feels helpless because he knows this is a battle I need to fight myself.

One of the event photographers chooses this awkward moment to ask for a picture of the two Barnard men and me.

"Miss Blum, do you mind joining them?"

I can't exactly refuse. Lee pulls me to his side and we plaster smiles on our faces. The elder Stanley rests his cold hand on my lower back. It feels like being touched by a snake.

Perhaps he lacks a heart after all.

The photographer snaps his pictures and thanks us.

I walk over to Dad and give him a hug. Lee follows behind and stops a few feet away to give us privacy.

"I'll tell your mother not to wait up for you tonight." Dad makes a subtle wink only I can see. "I'm sure Archie will fill in Rose with all the gossip. I don't have to tell you how excited your mom will be to meet him tomorrow. You and Lee will be the talk of the town."

I sigh. "Then it's a good thing I'm going back to Aspen soon."

Dad rubs his hand over my shoulder. "Speaking of Aspen, you might want to check your bid before you go. Unless you want strangers in the house."

To Lee he says, "Come over for lunch tomorrow. My wife will be disappointed she missed meeting you tonight."

"Thank you. I'd love to join you." Lee shakes his hand again.

The two of them standing together, chatting, warms my heart.

Lee weaves our fingers together when he takes my hand. "Ready?"

"One quick stop." I direct us to the silent auction lots and find the condo.

"Drats." Someone has outbid me.

I scribble a higher dollar amount on the next open line. "Take that, paddle two-seventy-two. You're a big loser."

Lee's deep laugh rumbles his chest against my back.

"What's so funny? Do you want some stranger invading my condo?"

"That's not your condo. It's mine." He flips over his name tag to reveal two-seventy-two on the reverse. "You called me a loser."

"We've been bidding against each other all evening?" Ours are the only two paddle numbers on the page after the third bid.

"At least it's for a good cause." He chuckles again. "Now no stranger will be rifling through either of our stuff."

I love it when he says words like we and our.

"Ready?" He holds out his hand.

"So ready."

TWENTY-SIX

STAN

THE SILK AND wool blend of my tux isn't itchy, but I squirm inside the confines of my monkey suit. My bowtie feels tighter around my neck. I stick a finger between my collar and skin to create more space before untying and letting my tie hang loose around my neck. The elevator takes forever to arrive in the lobby.

Staying in the same hotel as the event makes convincing Sage to join me in my room a much easier argument than yesterday.

I feel uncomfortable in my skin tonight. It's not only the suit suffocating me.

My heart races after confronting my father. I gave back my watch. I love that watch.

I rub my wrist. I have a permanent groove and a tan line where it sat for years.

"We left before dinner." She sighs as her stomach growls.

"We could go back and spend more time with my father." I lean against the side of the elevator. "Or we could order room service."

"Let's order room service. I wonder if they still have chicken tenders on the menu." She grins at the thought of fried boneless chicken the way some women would get excited about dressing up for a glamorous gala.

I open the door to my suite and Sage walks to the huge window overlooking the dark lake. "I feel like I'm on the edge of the world."

I turn on the bedside lamp, creating a single pool of light in the room. I'm torn between caging her against the window, showing her with my body what my words so epically got wrong, or trying the talking thing again.

"Sage." I step closer and rest my back against the glass next to her.

Her forehead presses against the window, but she shifts her eyes to see me. "Lee."

"I messed up on the Fourth. Tess and her crass description of us isn't what we're about."

"You didn't create an elaborate plan involving lists and secret pacts in order to get into my knickers?" She shifts again to stare at the dark water below us.

"No and yes."

She rolls her head on the window and then twists her body to face me. "Which is the no?"

"Don't be mad."

"Don't turn out to be an asshole and I won't have a reason to be mad." She tries to cross her arms, but I take her hands in mine.

"I added you to the list because I couldn't stand the thought of another man dating you, let alone touching you. When I did it, I didn't have a plan. At all. It was the start of training and the list came up. I was still pissed about Landon and added your name to keep the rest of the trolls away."

"Feeling possessive were you?"

I grumble and feel the vibration low in my chest. "A little. I also knew I had no claim on you. Nor should I. The man downstairs instilled a lot of strange values in me over the years, including some pretty twisted ones about emotions."

"Is that why you studied psychology?"

"Probably. Didn't really help me get in touch with my own feelings, though." Letting go of her hand, I brush my hand through my hair.

"Looking for the ghost of buns past?" She sweeps her fingers over the short hair on the side of my head.

"You can let it go now. It's gone."

"Would it be weird of me to say I missed it?" She tugs on the longer strands on the top. The gesture reminds me of how she pulled my hair during sex.

I move her hand and lace my fingers with hers. "I'm trying to apologize and you're distracting me."

"Okay, apologize."

"The smoothie bet was part of a master plan." I give her a sheepish smile and wait for her reaction.

"I knew it!" She pokes my chest. "I've seen you drink green smoothies before. The stakes were too high."

"Then why did you go along with it?"

"I was curious."

"About?"

"I wanted to see what dating you, even fake dating you would involve."

"You did? Does that mean your feelings for me weren't completely neighborly?"

She clears her throat and stares at our reflections in the window. "Perhaps. After Landon, I had rules and boundaries. You fell on the wrong side of them."

"I still don't know why you bothered with him."

"I never thought I stood a chance with you."

Her words are like a soft slap, but they still sting. "That's ridiculous. I'm the one who should feel unworthy. You're beautiful and have a huge heart. You come from an amazing family. You volunteer—"

She cuts me off. "Lee?"

"Yes?"

"Don't ever think you're not worth love." She presses her hand against my chest above where my heart thumps.

"I love you."

She responds by kissing me, her arms around my neck, and her body pressed as close as possible to mine. I need her to tell me she loves me. I can feel it in her kiss, but I need to hear the words.

"I love you," I repeat against her lips.

"I love you, Lee."

Her words permeate my skin, sinking into my bones and flowing through my blood, becoming part of me.

Nothing else needs to be said.

Flipping our positions so her back rests against the glass, I grind myself against her. I roam her body with my hands, squeezing and cupping her breasts. I grab her arse and hip, shifting her legs open to settle between her thighs. It's not enough.

I lift her, bracing her weight between my hips and the glass. The fabric of her dress gets in the way. I search for a zipper on the back while she sucks on the skin of my neck.

"You look stunning in this dress tonight, but I need it off of you now before I rip it."

She pauses and laughs. "It's my sister's. Rip it and she'll never forgive you. The zipper's on the side."

Pushing her fingers out of the way, I tug down the zipper. It's not enough. I set Sage on her feet and pull the offending material over her head.

She stands before me wearing only a small pair of black lace knickers and her heels.

"Fuck me," I whisper. My Colorado hippie girl is the sexiest thing I've ever seen. "Please tell me the heels are yours."

With a giggle, she replies, "By the look in your eyes right now, I'm never taking them off."

Lifting her arms above her head, I pin her to the glass. "I'm the luckiest man in the world."

"Prove it." She fingers the fly of my suit pants, brushing against my erection.

I'm momentarily frozen. I want to fuck her right here, but I also want to make love to her slowly on the bed, taking hours to draw out her pleasure until she begs.

"We have all night," she whispers.

"It's not enough time. I'm going to need forever for everything I have planned for us." I nip at her earlobe. "So answer my question. Fast or slow?"

Her eyes sparkle with wicked ideas. "Let's go fast."

I shrug off my suit jacket and toe off my shoes. She unbuckles and unzips me while I undo the studs and cuffs of my shirt. Everything gets tossed to the floor next to her dress.

"Turn around," I whisper. "Put your hands on the glass."

In her heels, her hips line up with mine perfectly. I reach into my wallet for a condom. Her eyes track my movements in the glass.

Slipping my fingers between her legs, I find her open and ready for me. I slide against her slick skin, teasing us both, before shifting and pressing the tip inside of her. I slowly thrust my hips, allowing her body to adjust. When my hips finally rest against her arse, I pull out and thrust with more force.

Our eyes lock in the window for a minute. I can see our

bodies coming together and her small breasts bounce and press into the glass with my thrusts.

Given the height of the hotel tower and location, unless someone is out on the lake with binoculars, no one can see us.

She closes her eyes and moans.

"Keep your eyes open, *liefie*. I want you to see how I love you."

Resting her head on my shoulder, she stares into my eyes through the reflection. "It's . . . I need . . ."

I cup one breast and slide her nipple between two fingers. My other hand drops to the top of her thighs right above where we're joined. Finding her clit, I press my thumb against it.

It's all she needs to fall apart in my arms. Between soft pants, she whispers, "I love you, Lee."

Those words are everything to me. I lose what little control I clung to and pull her hips back, pounding into her while she braces herself on the window.

I close my eyes, lost in the tight feeling of her pulsing around me. I open them again right as I come to find her smiling at me, nothing but love and lust in her eyes.

My own aftershocks spread through my body and I collapse against her. We tumble to the floor. I carefully remove the condom before sprawling out beside her on the carpet.

She spoons herself against me and we lie there staring out at the darkness.

I could fall asleep right here. My heavy lids close and I slowly force them open.

Sage's stomach growls again and she shakes with laughter.

"What are you thinking about?" I pull my fingers through the tangled strands of her hair.

"Chicken tenders." She giggles more. "It's embarrassing. I should be thinking about how blissed out I am and how amazingly, beyond the stars in love with you I am."

"Are you both of those things?" I kiss the top of her shoulder.

"Very much." She shifts to face me, tucking her head under my chin. I smell her lavender and honey scent. "And starving."

With a pat to her arse, I stand, holding out my hand for her to get up. "Let's order food."

A little while later we're wrapped in fluffy white robes and sitting in the middle of the enormous white bed surrounded by a feast fit for a toddler. We have chicken tenders, macaroni and cheese, mini hamburgers, and the best part, s'mores still warm and gooey.

"Here, try one." She holds out a breaded chicken strip dipped in some sort of sauce.

I take a bite.

"It's the most amazing chicken I've ever eaten." I grin happily at her.

"Can we never leave this room?" She sighs and chomps on another piece of chicken.

"Don't you miss the mountains? And the stars at night?" I've been here for seventy-two hours and I cannot wait to get home.

She leans against me. "I do."

"When can you leave?" Picking up the empty plates, I set them on the cart before returning to lie beside her.

"Can you delay your flight? I'll change mine and we'll catch an afternoon flight tomorrow to Denver. We can leave right after lunch. With my family."

"I'm looking forward to meeting your mom."

"Said no man ever." She kisses my cheek.

"I'm being honest. I haven't had a family most of my life."

"Careful what you wish for. Mine is loud and crazy."

"If they're anything like you, I'll love them."

She kisses my mouth and I taste honey. I slip my tongue

past her lips and lean her back into the pillows.

We make love slowly and with the lights on.

Afterward, she's sprawled across me, tracing the lines of my tattoo.

"I've never asked you what your tattoo is. I can tell it's tribal, but does it have special meaning?"

"It's a Zulu shield."

She freezes and then snorts. "Never, ever tell my mother that."

"Why?"

"Long story."

"We have all the time in the world." As I jokingly say the words, I know I want them to be true. I want forever with this woman.

"We also have puppies waiting for us at home." She's trying to distract me with thoughts of adorable puppies. It works. For now. Someday I'll find out the Zulu story and all her secrets.

Even if I have to make ridiculous bets to get what I want.

EPILOGUE

ONCE WE'RE ON the plane, I text with Zoe about Hunter and Nell. She assures me they're not going through separation anxiety and eating their feelings. This is the first time we're leaving them for more than a few hours. I don't believe her.

"What's wrong?" Lee asks.

"Zoe says the dogs are fine. I'm not sure if she's lying because I'm at JFK and boarding a million hour flight to South Africa. Or if everything is okay."

"Everything is fine. The dogs will be fine. They'll miss you and pine, but they're dogs. Think of how excited they'll be when we get home in two weeks?" Lee pats my hand.

"How long is this flight again?" I ask, adjusting my seat and pushing all my buttons. I feel like a kid on Christmas.

"You'll be fine." Lee's tone tells me I'm pushing some of his buttons, too.

"That doesn't answer my question." I tried to figure it out, but with the stopovers and time changes and hemisphere changes, I gave up. All I know is it's long.

"Longer than you'd think, but shorter than a day."

"Barely." We're flying halfway around the world to Cape

Town. Three continents, an ocean, a sea, and the equator will all be crossed before we get to Lee's hometown. How we ever managed to meet in this vast world blows my mind.

Then again, everything about the past year is unbelievable. Our fun walk to raise money for Elizabeth's ranch was a huge success and even got national media attention because some pop singer joined with her asthmatic pug in a stroller. I wrote my first five figure check to cover operating expenses. Elizabeth asked if I wanted the goat barn named after me. I declined and suggested another name. The Lee Barnard Goat Barn has a lovely ring to it.

"We're in business class. You have your own pod with your own TV to watch all the movies and random shows you love. Maybe they have Outlander." He knows me so well. Turns out he doesn't have tens of millions in the bank like I do, but he has enough money to only fly business or first class.

"You're too far away. How are we supposed to join the mile high club when we can barely hold hands over this enormous console?" I pretend to struggle to reach his hand. He grabs mine and pulls me over the divider to kiss me soundly on the lips.

"Where there's a will, I'll figure out a way."

"I like your thinking, Lee."

He gives me a slow lopsided smile. "What ever happened to Stan?"

"I prefer you as a Lee. Now that I've met the real Stanley, I don't want you to ever think I see similarities."

"Thank you for saying I'm nothing like my father."

"You're nothing like your father." Wrinkling my nose, I shake my head.

"I love you." His love shines in his eyes.

"I love you, too."

"When did your feelings change for me?" We've never talked

about the big shift from neighbors to friends to lovers.

I share the first thing that comes into my mind. "The night you hurt your ankle, you told me you'd never let me go as you fell asleep on my sofa."

He widens his eyes in surprise. "I said that out loud?"

I bob my head, grinning. "I blamed the drugs and your ramblings about Landon."

With a sexy growl, he lunges across the divider. His hand cups my neck below my hairline as he stares into my eyes. "Any man would be a fool not to hold onto you with everything he has."

He kisses me until I'm breathless.

"I should know. I almost lost you." He kisses me again, invading and claiming my mouth with his tongue. "I'm never letting you go."

"Ever?" Even my voice is breathless.

"Never. You faced the devil for me. You're coming with me to the other side of the world to meet my mum. You're the best thing in my life."

I blink and tears pool in my eyes.

"You're my everything." He emphasizes his words with light kisses. "I love you, *liefie.*"

"I love you." All sense of our surroundings leaves me as I give up my seat and crawl into his lap. His hands weave through my hair, pulling me closer. Our smiles and giggling make kissing difficult, but we can't stop trying.

When his fingers brush along the outside of my breast, reminding me of the first time he touched them, also in public, my fog of lust clears. His other hand rests on my hip and bottom. My fingers are gliding over his abs underneath his T-shirt.

A polite cough snaps me further out of my haze.

"*Jislaik,*" Lee mumbles against my mouth. "*Eishh.*"

Too embarrassed to face the flight attendant, I tuck my head into his shoulder.

"Everyone needs to be in their own seats with their seat belt buckled for take off, miss."

Lee says something rapid to her in Afrikaans before giving me a little tap on the hip. I duck my head and scoot back to my own seat, quickly fastening my seat belt. The inflight magazine has a fascinating article about the Zulus and I bury my nose in it, hiding my burning cheeks.

Lee curls his long finger over the magazine's spine and tugs. "She's gone now."

"What did you tell her? What did she say?" I refuse to lower the magazine. I can hear the smirk in his voice. I don't need to see it.

"I told her you are a wild sex fiend and I've never seen you before." He can't even finish his sentence before I've tossed the magazine at his head.

His laughter earns an over the seat stare from the older man in the row ahead of us.

"Shh."

I widen my eyes and make an O with my lips. "Seriously?"

"She's checking the back of the plane for an empty seat in coach for you right now." He snorts and bursts back into laughter when I pull the blanket over my head.

"You started it." He tugs the quilted fabric away from my face.

"You were in my lap, *skattebol*. Not the other way around. I even have my buckle fastened." He points to his lap where he's partially tenting his pants.

"Not helping! I'm going to die of embarrassment before we even take off. I'm never going to survive all the way to Africa."

The man in front of us coughs and clears his throat. Even

his judgmental body sounds don't stop Lee's laughter.

"God, I love you, Gertrude Sage."

"I want to die. Good-bye, world." I fold the blanket back over my hair and pin it down with my arms.

He manages to squeeze his face under the blanket near my face. After gently kissing my cheek, my jaw, and the skin below my ear, he whispers, "I apologized for making out with my future wife and being disrespectful to our fellow passengers. She suggested we wait until they dim the cabin lights and to stay under a blanket."

He nips my ear lobe and his breath warms my skin. Then he's gone.

I sit under the blanket, cocooned in warm darkness that smells like him, digesting his words.

Flipping down the blanket, I stare at him. "Did she really give you suggestions on how to make out on a plane?"

He nods, his tongue toying with the edge of his mouth.

I rest my head on the seat back.

"That's your only question, *liefie,* my love?"

I close my eyes, letting my smile spread across my face. I try to fight it, to resist grinning. Pressing my lips together, I nod.

"Are you sure?" He's moved closer and I can smell his minty breath and soapy skin.

I nod again, still fighting my grin.

His lips brush against the corner of my mouth. I'm certain he can see the tremble from my effort not to smile. "My love."

I peek at him through my lashes. His love fills his eyes and his own smile brightens his entire face.

"Is this going to be like when we got the puppies? Zero discussion and you making all the decisions? A little presumptuous, given you haven't asked."

"Soon," he whispers before kissing me again.

A NOTE FROM DAISY

Thank you for reading!

This is my first standalone novel outside the Modern Love Stories and Wingmen worlds. I had a ton of fun writing these characters and exploring a new setting. I hope you enjoyed Stan the Man Bun and Sage's story.

ABOUT DAISY

DAISY PRESCOTT IS the USA Today bestselling author of contemporary romantic comedies, including Modern Love Stories, the Wingmen series, and the Love with Altitude series.

Daisy currently lives in a real life Stars Hollow in the Boston suburbs with her husband, their rescue dog Mulder, and an indeterminate number of imaginary house goats. When not writing, she can be found in the garden or kitchen, lost in a good book, or on social media, usually talking about hot, bearded men and sloths.

www.daisyprescott.com

www.twitter.com/Daisy_Prescott

www.facebook.com/daisyprescottauthorpage

www.instagram.com/daisyprescott

ACKNOWLEDGMENTS

I'm thankful most of all for my readers. Thank you for buying, reading, reviewing and sharing my books.

Stan has his own book because of passionate readers who asked about the hot bartender in *Take for Granted*. Like John Day as the hot neighbor in *Geoducks*, I'd never planned to write a book for the man bun sporting rugby player until readers passionately requested more. I hope this book lived up to your fantasies!

Big thanks to my husband for always being my biggest supporter and first reader. His input makes my heroes better in so many ways.

Stanley is South African because of Debbie Prins. When he first appeared in the short story *Take for Granted*, he was from New Zealand. When I began thinking about writing a novel starring Stan, I switched his nationality. Debbie helped bring him to life with her input on all things Afrikaans and South Africa. I am truly grateful for her feedback and research, especially on the swearing and baked goods.

Julia Kent and Helena Hunting read early drafts of this. I'm lucky to have their input, and even luckier for their friendships. A big thank you to the lovely Natasha Boyd for her feedback and encouraging words.

Big thanks to all the authors of the Friends with Benefits books in this series for their cheerleading, support, and wicked smart brains. I've had the best time working with you and sharing our mad love for Chuck.

To all my readers in Daisyland, thank you for continuing to

support and champion my books! You are always a highlight of my day.

To the bloggers and reviewers, who tirelessly promote authors and books because they're passionate about reading, thank you for all of your support and enthusiasm.

Gratitude to my editor Melissa Ringsted for correcting grammatical sins, and to Marla Esposito and Elli Reid for proofreading. Thank you for the beautiful cover, SM Lumetta.

I'm blessed to have Fiona Fischer and Jessica at Inkslinger PR on my team. Thanks for keeping me focused and seeing the forest through the trees. As always, thank you to my agents, Flavia Viotti and Meire Dias at Bookcase Literary Agency, who continue to share my work with the world.

Most of all, thank you you for leaving a review or telling a friend about my books.

Hearing from my readers is the best part of publishing. I can be reached on social media or at *daisyauthor@gmail.com*.

xo

Daisy

77707505R00135

Made in the USA
Lexington, KY
01 January 2018